# The Trespasser

## AMISH COUNTRY BRIDES

Jennifer Spredemann

Published in Indiana by *Blessed Publishing*.

www.jenniferspredemann.com

All Scripture quotations are taken from the King James Version of the Holy Bible.

Cover design by iCreate Designs ©

ISBN: 978-1-940492-41-4
10 9 8 7 6 5 4 3 2 1

# BOOKS by JENNIFER SPREDEMANN

*Learning to Love – Saul's Story*
(Sequel to Chloe's Revelation)

## AMISH BY ACCIDENT TRILOGY
*Amish by Accident*
*Englisch on Purpose* (Prequel to *Amish by Accident*)
*Christmas in Paradise* (Sequel to *Amish by Accident*) (co-authored with Brandi Gabriel)

## AMISH SECRETS SERIES
*An Unforgivable Secret - Amish Secrets 1*
*A Secret Encounter - Amish Secrets 2*
*A Secret of the Heart - Amish Secrets 3*
*An Undeniable Secret - Amish Secrets 4*
*A Secret Sacrifice - Amish Secrets 5* (co-authored with Brandi Gabriel)
*A Secret of the Soul - Amish Secrets 6*
*A Secret Christmas – Amish Secrets 2.5* (co-authored with Brandi Gabriel)

## AMISH BIBLE ROMANCES
*An Amish Reward*
*An Amish Deception*
*An Amish Honor*
*An Amish Blessing*
*An Amish Betrayal*

# Unofficial Glossary
## of Pennsylvania Dutch Words

*Ab im kopp* – Off in the head, crazy

*Ach* – Oh

*Aldi* – Girlfriend

*Bann* – Shunning

*Boppli/Bopplin* – Baby/Babies

*Bruder* – Brother

*Daed/Dat* – Dad

*Dawdi* – Grandfather

*Dawdi Haus* – A small house intended to house parents or grandparents

*Denki* – Thanks

*Der Herr* – The Lord

*Dochder* – Daughter

*Dummkopp* – Dummy

*Englischer* – A non-Amish person

*Fraa* – Wife

*G'may* – Members of an Amish fellowship

*Gott* – God

*Grossdochder* – Granddaughter

*Mammi* – Grandmother

*Gut* – Good

*Jah* – Yes

*Kapp* – Amish head covering

*Kinner* – Children

*Mamm* – Mom

*Mammi* – Grandmother

*Mei fraa* – My wife

*Ordnung* – Rules of the Amish community

*Rumspringa* – Running around period for Amish youth

*Schatzi* – Sweetheart

*Schweschder(n)* – Sister(s)

*Sehr gut* – Very good

*Wunderbaar* – Wonderful

# Author's Note

The Amish/Mennonite people and their communities differ one from another. There are, in fact, no two Amish communities exactly alike. It is this premise on which this book is written. I have taken cautious steps to assure the authenticity of Amish practices and customs. Old Order Amish and New Order Amish may be portrayed in this work of fiction and may differ from some communities. Although the book may be set in a certain locality, the practices featured in the book may not necessarily reflect that particular district's beliefs or culture. This book is purely fictional and built around a fictional community, even though you may see similarities to real-life people, practices, and occurrences.

We, as *Englischers*, can learn a lot from the Plain People and their simple way of life. Their hard work, close-knit family life, and concern for others are to be applauded. As the Lord wills, may this special culture continue to be respected and remain so for many centuries to come, and may the light of God's salvation reach their hearts.

# ONE

Kayla Johnson squinted to see through the windshield as her wipers attempted to keep up with the torrential downpour assaulting her vehicle. But even with the wipers at full speed, that proved to be a challenge. She wasn't even sure where she and Bailey were exactly, but they'd crossed the state line from Kentucky into Indiana about an hour ago, or so it seemed. She distinctly remembered the 'Welcome to Indiana' sign just as they'd crossed the bridge over the gigantic Ohio River.

Perhaps she should pull over somewhere and wait out the storm. She couldn't tell if she was even going the right way, since her GPS had lost its signal several miles back. She figured it was due to the storm raging outside. How long would this last? *Now* she understood when people mentioned the storms in the Midwest. This was downright terrifying.

As if on cue, a streak of lightning touched down just off to the left. Not even five seconds later, thunder shook her car. A shiver raced up her spine.

"I'm scared, Mommy," Bailey whimpered from her booster seat in the backseat.

*Me too.* "It's okay, baby. Mommy's going to pull off up here." She'd hoped to find a motel or a fast food restaurant, but who knew how far she was from one. The last town had several, but she'd spotted them before the sky began dumping buckets of water. She hadn't expected *this*. If she'd known this was coming, she would have reserved a hotel room in the last town, and she and her five-year-old daughter would be safe and sound, curled up under the covers watching a family-friendly movie.

She flipped on her signal and maneuvered onto the next street. Great, no lines to even mark the road? She must be out in the middle of nowhere. The vehicle crawled at a snail's pace as she struggled to see the road ahead of her. It seemed to be at least a couple of inches deep in water. They really needed to get out of this. Was that a little store up ahead? She couldn't be sure since there were no lights on, but they were probably closed. 'Yoder's Country Market' the sign on the small white building read. *Yoder.* Wasn't that an *Amish* name? As she pulled into the drive, she discovered a chain-link fence surrounding the parking lot. Definitely closed.

She sighed.

"I need to go to the bathroom," Bailey whined.

"Okay. I think there might be a house down this driveway. We'll stop and ask to use their restroom." She drove along what appeared to be a fenced pasture. Or was it a small pond? It was difficult to tell with all the water everywhere.

Her cell phone began vibrating. No doubt another storm warning. She briefly glanced at it. *Flash flood warning.* Great. Perhaps the residents would allow her and Bailey to stay a while. She hoped so, because being out in this weather set her nerves on edge.

She pulled up to a large white two-story house. Should she just stop in front, or find a place to park out of the rain? She opted for the latter when she noticed a couple of structures independent of the house. A barn and another outbuilding of some sort. She slowly crept up to the smaller structure, hoping there was an empty spot large enough to house her vehicle.

Thunder rumbled overhead once again.

"Please, Mommy! I gotta go!"

"Okay, baby." As soon as she pulled under the outbuilding's roof, she could see clearly enough to park. She spotted a hitching post. *This must be where they park the buggies.* Except, there were no buggies present. Perhaps they were in the massive barn. Hopefully, the owners wouldn't mind her parking her car there.

Kayla opened the door, then went to release Bailey from her booster seat. "Do you think you can wait for Mommy to find the umbrella? It's just in my suitcase."

"I think so. But please hurry!" Bailey slid out of the car, then bounced up and down.

"I will." She quickly popped the trunk open and rifled through her clothing. She grabbed a comfortable change of clothes for each of them, just in case they were allowed to stay a while. "Okay. You ready to make a run for the door?"

"Yep."

"One. Two. Three." With the clothing tucked under her arm, she held the umbrella in one hand and Bailey's hand in the other, then made a mad dash for the front door.

"Whew!" She glanced down at her jeans near her ankles. They were completely soaked. It was a good thing she'd thought to grab extra outfits for the two of them. It would take a while for her tennis shoes to dry, however.

She knocked on the door loudly so it would be heard over the pounding rain. Didn't it ever let up? It seemed not.

No answer. She knocked again, harder this time.

"Mommy!" Bailey bounced.

"Okay, okay. I don't think anyone's home. I don't feel right just going inside."

"Maybe no one lives here anymore or they're on vacation like us." Bailey turned the knob, and the door opened. She rushed inside before Kayla could stop her.

"Bailey!"

"I have to go potty!"

Kayla gingerly stepped into the house and looked around the dark room. Indeed, it appeared empty. "Hello? Is anybody home?"

No answer.

"My daughter needs to use the restroom," she called out, stepping further inside. "Hello!"

Silence answered back. No one was home.

"Okay, we'll quickly find the bathroom, then we'll leave." She felt for a light switch but found none. *Oh, yeah. Amish. No electricity.*

A flash of lightning illuminated what appeared to be the living area, revealing sparse furniture covered in white sheets. It was as though the occupants had

5

moved. But why would they leave the door unlocked?

"Where will we go?" Bailey's frightened voice commanded her attention once again.

"I don't know, baby. Maybe...let's just find the bathroom so you don't pee your pants." She released a sigh of relief. If nobody was home, if the house was unoccupied, perhaps hunkering down here for an evening might be an option. But still, it wasn't her home. And how would she feel if a stranger occupied her place of residence in her absence? Not that she currently had a place of residence.

She walked through the darkened home. Thankfully, it wasn't pitch black. There should be a lantern somewhere, shouldn't there be? Perhaps not, if the owners no longer occupied the place. She scolded herself for not thinking to grab the flashlight out of the glove compartment. Of course, she hadn't expected to find a dark empty house. She'd run back out to get it if buckets of water weren't dumping from the sky.

She felt her way into the main living area until her eyes adjusted. Another flash of lightning revealed a kitchen off to one side. As she walked further inside the home, a quick perusal indicated a bedroom stood off to the other side, along a short hallway that led to stairs. Perhaps the bathroom adjoined the bedroom.

She peered inside the empty room. No, it didn't appear to.

"I found it!" Bailey hollered.

A door slammed shut. Whew! At least now she didn't have to worry about Bailey having an accident.

Once her eyes adjusted a little more, she spotted a lone lantern on a small table. Oh, good, a book of matches sat next to it. She quickly removed the hurricane glass, turned up the wick, then swiped a match to light it. A soft glow dispelled the darkness.

Fortunately, she'd come from a family of campers, so she was familiar with lighting lanterns, setting up tents, chopping wood, kindling a campfire, and other outdoor skills. Sadness filled her as she thought of Mom and Dad and all the wonderful times they'd spent camping. They'd passed away much too early. Did anyone survive cancer these days? It seemed not.

She briefly toured the lower level of the home with the lantern in hand, noting a few bedrooms. Two of them had lone beds in them, one covered by a quilt and the other with a plain comforter. Would the owners mind if she and Bailey occupied the rooms for a night? Since there seemed to be no one around to ask, she'd have to take a chance. What other choice did they have?

Thunder roared outside once again along with

pounding rain. It appeared they wouldn't be going anywhere anytime soon. Not with all the flash flood warnings and lightning strikes. It just wasn't safe. Or smart.

Had Someone up above provided this shelter from the storm? It was possible, she supposed, but definitely not probable. The Man Upstairs didn't care about her or Bailey, she'd been certain of that since she first discovered her pregnancy. And then she'd lost both parents.

No, it certainly wasn't God. Finding this place had been pure luck, plain and simple.

# TWO

Silas Miller dashed for the shelter of the barn. He hated to take Strider out in this weather, but he needed to check the Yoders' gutters to make sure they were free of debris. It was times like this he was thankful his Amish community allowed enclosed buggies. The nearby Swiss Amish district, nicknamed the Swissies by local Plain folks, only utilized open-top carriages. He couldn't imagine weathering this menacing storm with a simple umbrella as protection. At least he was protected from the elements.

He quickly harnessed Strider, moved him between the traces, making sure to guide them into their proper places, and then pulled the leather reins into the buggy's cab. Fortunately, his horse loved the rain. Unfortunately, Strider did not love thunder and lightning.

Strider whinnied, excited to be leaving his barn

stall, no doubt. He might have a change of mind once they got out onto the road and encountered a loud crash of thunder like the one several minutes ago. Maybe *Der Herr* would have mercy on poor Strider and hold off the lightning until they arrived at the Yoders'. He'd pray for that.

"Come on, boy. We won't be out too long, but it'll be enough to invigorate you." He gave the lines a gentle shake, urging Strider to begin their three-mile journey.

It seemed like the rain had let up a tiny bit, but it still poured. He just hoped the driver of the car up ahead spotted him and slowed down. This road was quite narrow and, in some places, had no room to pull off to the side. He double checked to make sure his blinking lights were on. He pulled to the right as much as possible to allow the car to pass.

He sighed in relief once it did. Hopefully, no one else was crazy enough to be out in this weather. He wouldn't be either, but he'd promised Dan Yoder that he'd look after his place after their family had moved back to Pennsylvania. Dan, the minister of their district, had talked about selling the place on more than one occasion, but for whatever reason, it had yet to go up for sale. And for that, Silas was happy. He'd dreamed about having his own acreage, complete with a large barn, and a small store in the front, since he'd been finished with school. The Yoders' property would be the perfect place, but he was in no position finance-wise to buy it. Nowhere near, actually. But he had been saving his money. And praying that the house wouldn't sell to anyone else.

As he neared the two-mile mark, he noticed something up ahead. *Ach,* the creek had swollen considerably.

"Do you think we can do it, Strider?"

The horse lifted his head as though in agreement.

"Okay, but we'll have to be careful."

He approached the water cautiously and urged Strider along. "Come on, boy. You can do this." He slapped the reins a little firmer. "Let's go!"

The horse waded through the water adequately, but the buggy still weighed him down. Silas encouraged the horse again and glanced out the side flap. The water reached the middle of his buggy's wheel. If it were any higher, Strider wouldn't be able to pull through.

Once they were safely past the creek, he exhaled in relief. It proved to be swifter than he'd surmised. Getting back home would be a chore if the creek rose any higher. As a matter of fact, maybe he'd use the Yoders' phone shanty and leave a message on the line closest to his folks' place. That way, if they worried about him, they'd check the answering machine before heading out into the foul weather in search of him. Staying overnight at the Yoders' place would almost seem like a mini vacation. And he could dream of the future when he—*Gott* willing—owned the place. He smiled at the thought. *Jah*, that was what he'd do.

He stopped at the phone shanty at the end of the lane when he'd driven in, and left a message. Hopefully, *Mamm* wouldn't worry about him. Ten minutes later, he pulled into the drive. He led Strider to an empty stall in the barn, then filled a bucket with water and offered the horse some grain he kept stored in the corner.

He stood looking toward the house, waiting for a break in the rain. After a few minutes, he realized he might not get one. As a matter of fact, it was coming down even harder than when he'd pulled in. He was just glad he'd been able to arrive before the lightning struck. Now that Strider was securely in the barn, he'd settle in for the night. He'd have to wait until the rain died down a little bit to check the gutters.

He wished he'd thought to bring an umbrella. It certainly would have made his escape to the house a bit more pleasant. And dry.

Silas pushed the door open and immediately removed his boots. He paused for a moment, midstride as he walked through the living room. Had he heard something or was it just his imagination? It was difficult to determine above the rain pounding on the metal roof. He'd always loved the sound. How many nights had he fallen asleep to it?

He reached for the lantern on the table. Except it wasn't there. He could have sworn that he'd left it in the same place he always did—not that he'd ever really swear. As he allowed his eyes to adjust to the dim interior, he noticed something peculiar. Faint light seeped from the bedroom door, which seemed to be cracked open. The hairs on his arms raised. Was someone inside the house?

His heart began pounding. Who could be here? Dan Yoder hadn't said he was returning, so it must be an intruder. He quietly tiptoed toward the bedroom door, then put his ear to the crack. Sure enough, someone or something was in that bedroom.

All at once, he forced the door open and burst into the room. "What are you doing here?"

"Ah!" A young woman, who stood in only her undergarments, quickly pulled the bed quilt around herself.

*Jah*, that had been a mistake. Too bad he'd realized it

too late. His face burned. "I...I'm sorry...you just...uh, *jah*...I'll...I'll just go...out." He turned around as quickly as he'd entered. *Oh, man. What have I done?*

Silas paced the living room, trying to determine his next course of action. Had he *really* just burst in on a woman while she was changing? *Ach! Dummkopp.*

A few moments later, the woman—fully dressed now—walked into the room. "I'm sorry that you..." She shook her head. "This is a little awkward."

He nodded. *Jah*, it certainly was. He had no words.

"My daughter and I were out driving in the storm. She needed to use the facilities, so we stopped in here, thinking someone would be home. We'd only planned to use your restroom and then be on our way to search for a hotel, but they'd sent out flash flood warnings and my GPS lost its signal. And frankly, I don't even know where we are." She glanced toward one of the bedrooms. "My daughter is sleeping already. But we can leave if you'd like us to...uh, Mr. Yoder."

"Oh, I'm not Dan Yoder. My name is Silas Miller. I live down the road a spell. I'm tending Yoder's farm while he's gone."

"Oh, okay. When will he be back? Do you think he'd mind if we stayed the night? I didn't want to assume, but we really have no place to go."

"Not sure if he's coming back." He lifted his hat

and plowed his fingers through his hair. What should he do? He didn't want to kick this woman and her daughter out in the storm. But if they stayed here, where would *he* spend the night? He didn't relish the thought of sleeping in the barn with the mice.

"Do you want us to go?"

*In a word, yes.* But he wouldn't say that out loud. How could he kick them out when they didn't have any place to go? And in this storm. "The nearest hotel is about fifteen miles south of here." He shifted from one foot to the other. "But I reckon it would be all right if you stayed here."

She sighed, and he could almost feel her relief. "You don't know how glad I am to hear you say that. I'm not that confident driving in this kind of weather. I'm dreading going back out into that storm."

*Jah*, so was he. But he'd have to do it anyway. Because there was no way he was staying in this house with a woman present.

"I'm sorry. Did you come here in a buggy? I can't imagine in this weather. There were flash flood warnings going off earlier."

"*Jah*, we waded through the swollen creek."

"Did you...were you planning to stay the night here?"

"I was." He nodded. "But I can sleep in the loft."

"You mean, in the barn? Oh, no. I'd hate to make you do that. We can leave. Really. I'll just go wake Bailey up and—"

"No." He reached for her arm to stop her before she dashed to the bedroom to awaken the sleeping child. "That is not necessary. You may stay."

"If our staying means you have to sleep in the barn, then we'll have to leave." She glanced back toward the bedroom. "Bailey and I can share a room. You may have the other one."

The corner of his mouth twitched. "This house has seven bedrooms. I don't think *that* will be a problem." He sighed. "I cannot stay here in the same house as you and your *dochder*."

"I trust you."

"You don't even know me."

"You're right. But the fact that you have offered to stay in the barn tells me you're a gentleman." She shook her head. "Have you ever stayed in a hotel?"

He nodded.

"Well, this isn't much different. One building. Different rooms for strangers. And this time I'll be sure to close and *lock* my door." Her sheepish smile reminded him that he needed to apologize once again.

"About that. I didn't mean to...I had no idea you would be..."

"Yeah, can we just forget about that and put it behind us?"

Not likely. *Nee*, he wouldn't be forgetting the image of the beautiful *Englisch* woman any time soon. But he *should* really try. "*Jah*."

"Good." She looked around. "So, do you need anything from me? Are there blankets in the other rooms?"

"I will be fine, *denki*." He couldn't believe he was agreeing to this outlandish idea. What would *Mamm* think? Or Jerry Bontrager, his bishop? Or Brother Yoder? *Ach*, he must be *ab im kopp*.

"Great. Then I'll go check on Bailey, and head for bed." She nodded, then turned back around on her way toward the bedroom. "By the way, thank you for letting us stay here. You're a life saver."

# THREE

Kayla yawned as she sat up from the bed and stretched. She'd slept great with the rain pounding the roof all night long. When was the last time she'd slept so soundly? It must've been before Mom and Dad passed away. What was it about this place that settled her soul, brought a sense of peace to her heart, set her mind at ease?

The rain hadn't let up much. She pushed her phone's wake-up button to see the time. Seven o'clock. Bailey would likely be asleep for another half hour.

She tapped the weather app and pressed location to get the area's forecast. *Rexville, Indiana?* She'd never even heard of it. She briefly wondered if it had been named after a dog named Rex. Who knew? She frowned at her phone. Constant thunderstorms for the next week? And a one hundred percent chance?

Could they really tell? Thunder shaking the house made her believe so. How much water could one area take before everyone was swimming?

Shoot! When would she and Bailey be able to get back on the road? Not that they had anyplace special they'd needed to be at any particular time. But still. She didn't want to inconvenience Silas another night. And at some point in time, they needed to head to Pennsylvania.

Commotion sounded like it was coming from the living area. She sniffed the air. Did she smell coffee? And bacon? Just then, her stomach growled.

She made sure once again that her door was locked and closed. She quickly dressed and then left her room. She had smelled food, and did it ever smell good. She quickly tiptoed to Bailey's room and listened at the door. No sound, which meant she was still asleep.

She headed toward the delicious aroma.

"I see the bacon has called your name." Silas smiled, looking robust and handsome in his Amish attire this morning.

She smiled. "More like the coffee."

"I hope you're hungry. I made enough for all three of us."

"I'm starving. Thank you." She stared at Silas, standing at the stove with his back toward her. When was the last time someone had made her breakfast? It must've been Mom. Now, not only would her mother never cook for her again, they'd never share another meal together either. A wave of sadness washed over her at the realization. *I miss you, Mom.*

"I apologize." Silas distracted her melancholy thoughts. "I only have one coffee mug here and one plate. I don't eat here often and when I do, it's only me. There are usually plenty of eggs on hand due to the hens Dan Yoder left. I take most of the eggs home, but leave some here in case I get hungry. Good thing they'd been laying a lot lately."

"Have you eaten?"

"I have. And I've washed the coffee mug and plate if you'd like to use it before your *dochder* awakens."

Silas's thoughtful ways reminded her of Dad. He was always considerate of others' wellbeing. "Thank you. Yeah, that's a good idea. I have no doubt she'll wake up hungry."

She moved to the stove and poured coffee from a kettle. The kettle brought back memories of camping. She smiled, once again remembering the good times she'd shared with her parents.

He chuckled. "You better eat fast then."

"You're right."

She took a couple slices of bacon and some of the

scrambled eggs he'd made and placed them on her plate. Then she moved to what looked like a homemade loaf of bread and took a pre-cut slice. She slathered butter on it, which she suspected had been homemade as well. What a treat! It wasn't a five course meal, but Silas had gone over and above what she expected. She'd have to be sure to thank him again.

She eyed this mystery man in front of her. He looked to be a few years older than her, about the age of Bailey's father. His beard indicated that he was most likely married, but he didn't really act as though he were. She was quite certain he wouldn't have stayed the night if he were married, no matter how persuasive she'd been. She was pretty sure Amish men were the family type.

"Are you married? I mean, if you don't mind me asking. I noticed that you have a beard, and I know that means you're married, right?"

"You are partially right. *Jah*, most Amish require a man to grow a beard after he is married. But some of the Swiss Amish are not this way. Young men grow face hair as soon as they're able." He scratched his short beard and frowned. "I am not married anymore. My Sadie Ann passed on two years ago yet."

"Oh. I'm so sorry. You're not even that old, are you?"

"Twenty-five." He grimaced. "Death is not a respecter of age, unfortunately."

"No, it isn't. I'd thought my parents died early, but you..." She shook her head. "How old was your wife?"

"Twenty-one. We were expecting our first *boppli*, a little one. There were complications. Neither of them survived. It was *Gott's* will." His eyes briefly glassed over and then he shook his head, as though he were experiencing the deep pain that accompanied losing a loved one, but was trying to move past it.

"I'm so sorry for your loss. It must have been difficult for you."

"*Jah*, it was. But I was not a stranger to death. My best friend drowned when I was nineteen."

She gasped. "That's terrible. Yet, you're still Amish?"

"I do not understand what you mean by that. Why would I *not* be?"

"I hate God for what He's taken from me," she spat out bitterly.

He shook his head. "You mustn't say that."

"But it's the truth. That's how I feel." Tears sprung to her eyes unwelcomed. "My mother was my best friend. She helped me so much when I went through my unplanned pregnancy and with raising Bailey. Why did He take her? Why didn't He let her live after I *begged* Him to?"

"Death is a part of life. We must accept *Gott's* will."

"I can't accept it. If He really is God, then He had the power to save my mom, yet He didn't. He knew how much I needed her. How much I loved her."

"I am sorry that you are hurting. *Gott* has a reason for everything. Sometimes He doesn't show us those reasons. That is when we have to trust that He knows best."

"What good reason could there possibly be for taking my mom from me early? Name one. Just one." She challenged.

"I do not claim to know *Gott's* reasons." He shook his head. "But I do know that He loves you."

She scoffed at his words. "Really? If that's what His love is like, He can save it for someone else. I sure as heck don't want it." She slightly regretted her last words. Would this Amish guy be offended at her use of 'heck'? Oh well, she'd already said it.

He frowned. "*Gott* sent Jesus to die for your sins, so you could have eternal life."

"See, that's what I mean. What kind of God makes His own Son suffer?"

"One who loves you. One who knows there is no other way for people to escape Hell. One who knew the future and that His Son would rise from the dead. One who made you. One who can be trusted."

"I admit you offer a pretty good defense."

"I only say the truth. Maybe it can help you. *Gott* carries a lot of my burdens on His own shoulders. He gives me peace in my heart. He will do the same for you."

*Could He?* She dismissed the thought as quickly as it surfaced.

She sighed. "Can we change the subject? I'm not really comfortable talking about this." Yes, she was very obviously blowing him off. She wasn't willing to discuss religion at length with anybody. As a matter of fact, this was probably the most she'd ever spoken about spiritual things.

"Sure." He seemed disappointed. "What is your story? Where are you and your *dochder* traveling to? And why?"

She chuckled at his curiosity. She supposed she did owe him an explanation. Especially after commandeering the house. "Well, frankly, I could use some money. I'm hoping to get child support from Bailey's father. That is, if I can find him."

"Where does he live?"

"He said Pennsylvania. I hope he wasn't lying."

"When did you see him last?"

"About the time Bailey was conceived." She noticed his cheeks reddening when she'd said that.

Perhaps the Amish didn't talk openly about such matters. "I really thought he was a different kind of guy than what he turned out to be. I gave him my phone number and address. He promised to write or call. Never did. He was obviously only looking to have a good time. Why do guys have to be like that?"

"I don't know. But not all of us are that way." Silas frowned. "Does he know about his *dochder*?"

"I had no way to contact him. He claimed he didn't have a phone or email, and he didn't want to give me his address. That should have been a huge red flag right there. He was just duping me, sweet talking me so he could get what he wanted." She shrugged. "I was a naïve sixteen-year-old who thought she was in love and he took advantage of that. Not that it was *all* his fault."

"*Ach*, sixteen?" His eyes widened.

She laughed. "I actually told him I was eighteen because I suspected he was a few years older."

"Was he?"

"Yep."

"So how do you plan to find him?"

"I googled his name online and have a couple of leads to go on, but nothing really substantial. There was a lot less information than what I'd hoped for." She frowned. "It seems like Josiah Beachy isn't that popular of a name."

"Josiah Beachy?" His brow lowered.

"Yeah. I thought it was pretty cool since we met in Ocean City at the beach. You know, beach—Beachy. Didn't think I'd ever forget a name like that. Just a minute." She jogged to the bedroom and opened her wallet, pulling out the strip of black and white photos she and Josiah had taken at a photo booth. It was her only physical link to him other than Bailey. How many times had she taken them out and dreamed of a future with Josiah?

She returned and handed Silas the photo strip. "That's him."

He briefly glanced at the photos—his expression unreadable—and then handed them back.

They both turned at the sound of Bailey's footsteps. Kayla hid the photo strip behind her back, folded it, and tucked it into her back pocket.

"Mommy." She stopped at the entrance to the kitchen and stared wide-eyed at Silas. She beckoned her mother with her finger, and Kayla bent down so she could whisper in her ear. "I had an accident."

"Oh no. It'll be okay, sweetheart. We'll take care of it," she whispered back.

"Who is that man?"

Kayla smiled. "This is Silas. He lives down the road, but takes care of this house. Silas, meet my daughter, Bailey."

"*Gut* to meet you." He nodded. "I hope you like my breakfast."

"Mommy says I'm a good eater because I'm not picky."

Kayla nodded. "Yes, well, before you eat, you'll need a bath."

Silas began walking toward the door. He reached for the umbrella, then briefly turned back. "I'm going to check on my horse."

Bailey's eyes grew large. She had a fondness for animals. "You have a horse?"

"Yep. Strider used to be a racehorse, so he's real fast." He smiled.

Kayla reached for Bailey's hand. "Well, come on, Bailey. Let's take care of business so you can eat. And we'll let Mr. Silas take care of his chores too."

"Is it still raining?" Bailey squinted to try to see through the windows.

"Yep, it sure is. Can't you hear it?" Silas pointed to the roof.

Bailey nodded, but Kayla stared after the handsome widower that walked out the door.

"I like Mr. Silas, Mommy." Bailey echoed her sentiments.

"Yeah, me too."

# FOUR

Silas's heart pounded like crazy. He had to escape the house as quickly as possible, lest Kayla see the dismay on his face. Did his best friend *really* father a child out-of-wedlock just prior to his death? *Ach*, it couldn't seem possible.

Yet, Kayla's story did add up. The photos alone were proof positive. Also, her *dochder* seemed to be about the right age to have been conceived during their *rumspringa* trip—the last one before they decided whether to join the church or not. Except Josiah never made it home from Ocean City. He'd attempted to swim in the ocean, but drowned when the current proved too strong and carried him away. There hadn't been any lifeguards on duty that day.

Silas and his buddies, all except for Josiah, had returned home earlier than expected. He had been the one to break the devastating news to his best friend's folks. Now it seemed he'd have to break the heart-wrenching news to his *dochder* and widow—well, not his actual widow because they hadn't been married. But if Josiah had known, he certainly would have married this beautiful woman who'd evidently been carrying his child. It likely wouldn't have been too difficult of a decision, because he'd hinted of leaving the Amish before. An *Englisch boppli* and *fraa* would have sealed the deal and given him a solid reason to become *Englisch*. Not even the probability of a strained relationship with his folks would've prevented his departure.

Josiah had told him in confidence that he'd met someone during their trip and was smitten with her, but to go so far as to conceive a child with someone he'd only known a few days? *Ach*, Josiah! It was too bad that he'd never have an opportunity to know his own *dochder*. Or have a relationship with her mother. And Kayla thought she'd been lied to. Abandoned.

It was a tragedy all the way around, for sure and certain. What he wouldn't give to have his own *fraa* and *boppli* back. He'd never see them again this side of eternity, just like Kayla and her *dochder* would never see Josiah.

Once again, he'd be the bearer of bad news.

She said she'd come for child support. *Ach*, but

what if she was hoping to rekindle the relationship they'd once had? What if she desired to make a family with his best friend?

More broken dreams for this young woman who already seemed beaten down. How could he stand to deliver more bad news? She'd already said she'd hated *Gott*. He had no desire to give her another reason to turn against *Der Herr*. Now, she would realize that she came looking for Josiah for no good reason. And there would be no child support.

Silas felt like weeping for the woman. Because there was no doubt that was what she would do when she learned of the devastating news. Did she have no one else to turn to? It seemed so.

He stepped out of the barn and into the pouring rain, allowing it to thoroughly soak him. He looked toward Heaven and lifted his hands. "Why, *Gott*?"

# FIVE

Silas stepped back into the house and stood in the entryway.

Kayla gasped. "Oh, my goodness, Silas! You're drenched. I thought you took the umbrella with you."

He nodded. "I did. I needed a little refreshment."

"A little? You're soaked to the bone."

"*Ach.*" He waved his hand in front of his face. "I'll dry out."

"Would you like for me to find you a towel?"

"That would be *gut, denki.*"

A moment later, she handed him a towel that had obviously been line dried. Some folks preferred the fancy soft hotel towels, but Silas enjoyed the invigorating roughness of a towel hung out to dry in the wind and sun. He continued to soak up the water to which he'd subjected himself.

"I was hoping you could show me where the

washing machine is. I searched the house, but I couldn't find one." She frowned. "Or is there even one here? I'd guess the owners would have taken it with them."

"*Nee*, they had limited space. I think they planned to leave whatever's left to the next owners." He prayed it would be him. "If there is one still here, it's likely in the basement."

"Oh, I hadn't thought to check there."

"I can show you. Chances are, you'll need me to show you how it works too, *jah*?"

"I know how to operate a washing machine," she stated confidently.

"An *Amish* washing machine?"

"Is there a difference?"

He chuckled. "You'd better just let me show you."

"Maybe I should wash your clothes too." She stared at his still-soaked attire.

"I have no others here."

Bailey interrupted their conversation. "I like your breakfast, Mr. Silas!"

He glanced over at the table where she sat eating. *Ach*, now that he got a *gut* look at her, she did resemble Josiah. "*Denki*. I'm happy to hear that." He smiled.

"What does *denki* mean?"

"It means 'thank you.' It is an Amish word. But some people say it differently. Some people say *danke*."

She laughed. "It sounds like donkey."

He grinned. "I supposed it does, doesn't it?"

She nodded, then smiled. "*Denki*," she tried out the word. "Mommy, I know an Amish word now!"

Silas looked at Kayla, and they both shared a smile. "Yes, you do."

"Will you teach me more Amish words, Mr. Silas? And will you show me your horse when it stops raining?" Bailey's smile stretched wide across her face.

"*Jah*." He suspected her eyes would light up at the word.

"That means 'yes,' right?"

"*Jah*." He nodded with a smile.

"*Jah*," she tested her new word.

"I think it's time for my little Amish girl to finish her breakfast now," Kayla suggested.

Silas blew out a breath. If she only knew how true her words were. Her little girl was half Amish, and she didn't even realize it. "You ready to see about washing clothes now?"

"*Jah*, I'm ready." Kayla winked.

He chuckled, then led the way to the basement.

There was something different about Silas, but Kayla couldn't put her finger on it. Ever since he'd gone outside and come back soaked, he seemed...preoccupied, maybe? She couldn't be sure.

"Okay, here is the water." Silas carried a metal bucket down the steps. He dumped it into the wringer washer basin. "Now, put your laundry soap in."

"I don't have any." She frowned. Apparently, she hadn't thought very far.

He turned around, looking for something. He opened a container and scooped up something gray, then added it to the water.

"What is that?"

"Homemade soap. Many Amish make their own. You can use it for washing clothes, washing dishes, bathing." He shrugged. "It's good for everything. Now, add your clothes."

She did as instructed.

"Now pull that knob out."

She smiled when the agitator began spinning. "How long do we leave the clothes in for?"

"About five minutes should be *gut* enough."

She nodded.

"This will clean much better than your modern *Englisch* washing machines."

"English? I think my old washing machine was

American made, but I could be wrong."

He chuckled. "*Englisch* is the word we use for non-Amish folks. Some Amish up north call you Yankees."

"That's funny. You'll have to teach that one to Bailey." She stared at the clothes momentarily. "Speaking of Bailey, I should go check on her. Thank you for your help with the laundry."

"We're not done."

She frowned. "We're not?"

"No. I said it washed better. I didn't say it was easier or faster." He grinned.

"I gotcha. Okay, I'll be right back then."

After she had Bailey settled at the table practicing her letters with a pencil and a piece of paper she'd found, Kayla headed back down the stairs to the basement. This new adventure proved to be exciting, actually. It wasn't every day a hot Amish widower instructed her in the art of washing clothes old-fashioned style. She enjoyed being in Silas's company, but she had no clue if the feeling was mutual.

"Are they done?" she asked as she hit the bottom step.

"Another minute, I think."

"Okay."

He eyed her curiously. "Where did you come from? Where is your home?"

"Well, it *was* California. But since I don't really have any reason to stay there anymore with my parents gone, I figured I'd try something different." She shrugged. "If I can find Bailey's father, well...I don't really know. It would be nice if he could be part of her life, you know? Every child should have a father. I mean, even if he doesn't want to have anything to do with me." She sighed. "But, who knows? He might have a family now. What if he does? I don't even know how he'll feel if we just show up out of the blue. It could turn out badly."

He remained quiet. And there it was again. That awkwardness.

Did he grimace? She wished she knew what he was thinking.

"Is something wrong? I have this feeling..."

He gave a curt shake of his head, apparently not wanting to expound on his thoughts. "We will talk later after the little one goes to bed for the evening."

"For the evening? I'd hoped to get back on the road, if this storm would ever let up."

"You're not going anywhere, and neither am I. There is flooding in both directions. You will not be able to make it out to the main road, and I will not be able to make it home. I hope you two like eggs, because that's what we'll likely be eating for several days yet."

"Several days?"

"Well, if the weather report on that contraption of yours is right, then *jah*."

"I do have some snacks in the car."

"I could fetch them, along with whatever else you might need."

"Having our suitcases would be nice. Just be sure you actually use the umbrella this time, okay?"

He nodded. "I will get them then, when we are done here."

"Thank you, Silas. You have been very kind to Bailey and me."

He shook his head. "Any Amish person would do the same."

He reached for the knob on the machine and pushed it in, and the agitator stopped spinning. "Now, see that lever there?" He pointed to the top left of the machine.

"This one?"

"*Jah*. Turn it toward me, and those two round gadgets will start rolling. That is your spin cycle. It takes the water out of the clothes." He pulled a pillow case from the murky water and held it close to the spinning bars. "See? Feed it through like this. But take care not to trap your fingers inside if you'd like to keep them."

"That sounds ominous."

"It's no joke. It can be quite dangerous."

She blew out a breath. "Then I will be careful."

He did something to release the dirty water from the tub. She guessed the hose must run outside somewhere.

"Just let them fall into that tub there." Silas reached for the bucket. "I must get more water. It's a *gut* thing we have a full cistern right now." He disappeared up the stairs again.

*Cistern?*

A few moments later, he dumped a bucket of water into the large tub that the now-spun clothes fell into. "This is your rinse water. When you're done, turn that lever the opposite way, and feed them back into the other side."

He disappeared up the stairs again with the bucket, then promptly returned. "We will complete this process one more time with clean water to be sure and certain all the soap is out. Then, we can pin it on the line."

"Wow, you weren't kidding when you said it wasn't easier."

"No. But you will see how clean the clothes are, and how much more water this takes out. They'll dry faster on a windy day than with an electric dryer."

"Really? Wow." She ran the sheets and the few articles of clothing through as Silas had instructed. "Okay, now take your clothes off."

Silas stared back at her wide-eyed.

"Silas, you're soaking wet. Your clothes must be cold and heavy. Take them off so I can run them through the wringer."

He crossed his arms over his chest and shook his head.

She did admit to herself that she liked the way his wet shirt clung to his body, accentuating his muscular frame. "I'll turn around, for crying out loud. Besides, it's not as if you didn't barge in on me yesterday when I was changing." She turned her back to him then held her arm out for his clothes.

He grunted but then sighed in surrender. She smiled as she heard him removing his clothing, then felt his wet pants in her hand. She waited for his shirt, then proceeded to run them both through the wringer to remove the excess water. No doubt his clothing would be much more comfortable and lighter to wear once all the water had been squeezed out.

"Done." She handed his clothing to him, keeping her back to him. As soon as she was certain his pants were on, she turned around. She wouldn't miss the only opportunity she'd get to see Silas shirtless.

Wow, he looked even better without a shirt on than she'd imagined. The Amish obviously took manual labor seriously, and it definitely showed.

Silas cleared his throat as he finished buttoning his shirt.

Kayla's cheeks warmed when she realized that he'd noticed she'd been staring at him. She quickly turned around and grasped the other items they'd washed.

"These need to dry, but it's raining outside. How will we—" She stopped talking when she heard a squeaking sound.

Silas pulled on a rope that was connected to a pulley in the corner of the basement ceiling.

"Wow, the Amish think of everything. Drying clothes inside?"

He removed the clothespins from the cute little dress clothespin holder, then chuckled. "We've been doing this for hundreds of years, so I think we've learned a thing or two."

"I should say so." She couldn't get over this unique old-fashioned culture. Something about it felt very comforting. Or maybe it was Silas's gentle ways that seemed to set her mind at ease.

# SIX

Silas blew out a breath. The impending conversation with Kayla would most likely not be a pleasant one, and he'd been dreading what he had to tell her. He hated to be the one to dash her last hope. But remaining silent would be even worse. The truth was the truth, and there was no changing it. She needed to know the truth. She deserved to know the truth.

*Gott, please help me to deliver this news to Kayla. Give me the words to say.*

"I think she's finally down for the night." Kayla spoke softly as she entered the living room.

"Does it always take her this long to fall asleep?"

Kayla smiled. "It depends on how long her bedtime story is."

"I see."

He'd never had a chance to read a bedtime story to

his little one, would never get the chance. He forced his unexpected emotions into compliance and focused on the task at hand.

"Thank you for bringing her books in."

He nodded, then gestured toward the couch for her to sit down. "You are a good mom to Bailey."

Her brow lowered. "Do you think so? I try to be. But raising a child alone isn't for the faint of heart. I often feel inadequate."

"I think her father would be pleased."

"I don't know. Maybe I should have looked him up sooner, tried to find him. I hate the fact that she doesn't have a father figure in her life. My dad filled that role until he passed away. But I feel that she really needs that male presence in her life. I can only be so many things to her."

"*Jah*, I understand."

"So, what was it that you wanted to discuss?"

"I called Dan Yoder, the owner of this property."

Her mouth turned down. "He wants us to leave, right?"

"*Nee*. I asked him if he'd be willing to rent it out."

"Rent it out? To me? I'm not quite following your train of thought." She nodded. "Oh, wait, I see. Sure, I can pay for the nights Bailey and I stay here. We'd be paying at a hotel anyway. And this is more private."

"*Ach*, I am not speaking right. *Nee*, what I mean is, would you *like to* rent this house?"

"You mean, like for months? Or years? No. Remember I told you we were heading to Pennsylvania? We only stopped here because of the storm."

"*Nee*, it was not because of the storm." He shook his head. "*Der Herr* brought you here."

"*Der Herr*?"

"*Gott*."

"Silas…" She sighed.

*Ach*, he needed to just come out with it. "Josiah Beachy was my best friend. We grew up together in Pennsylvania before my family moved here."

Kayla's jaw dropped. "You know Josiah? My Josiah? Bailey's father?"

He nodded. "I did."

"Did? Are you not friends anymore?"

"Kayla." He sighed, then moved to sit next to her. He lightly touched her hand. He gentled his tone, hoping that would lessen the impact of his words. "Josiah died not two days after you saw him last."

*Ach*, saying the words aloud stirred up emotions he thought he'd long dealt with.

She stared at him, allowing the words to register in her mind.

He continued. "He went swimming in the ocean

and drowned. That is why he never contacted you."

Tears now filled her eyes, as he suspected they would. "Josiah is *dead*? I...I don't even know how to respond to that. Out of all the possible scenarios of what may have happened and why he'd rejected me, I never considered that he might no longer be alive. That's terrible. It's awful."

He wanted to rub her hand to comfort her, but held back. "He had just told me that he'd met a wonderful *Englisch* girl. He said he would write you, and if you'd responded to his letters, then he wouldn't join the Amish church yet but go find you instead."

"I don't...why?" She sobbed now, covering her face with both hands. "Why did he have to die?"

"I don't know. I asked the same question many years ago. We grew up together, went to school together. He was my closest friend. I hated returning home without him. I felt like I left a piece of me there at the beach." He touched her hand now, wishing he knew how to comfort her. When he'd lost his *fraa* and *boppli*, he'd mostly grieved alone.

"Now Bailey will never know her father. I'm glad I hadn't said anything to her about trying to find him. She would have been devastated." She forced away her tears. "Now, after traveling all this way... I guess I no longer have a reason to continue on to Pennsylvania."

"I'm sorry to deliver bad news."

"Silas, you have nothing to be sorry for."

"I am sorry that Josiah never got a chance to know he had a *dochder*. He would have been a *wunderbaar* father. When he'd said he'd met someone, I never realized that he meant he would go so far as to...well..." He swallowed. He shouldn't have gone there. Now, it was awkward.

"To conceive a child?" She finished his unspoken sentence. "We were young and, well, probably not all that wise. We let our emotions get the best of us, I suppose."

"*Jah*, that is easy to do."

"You sound like you speak from experience."

He shook his head. "*Nee. Mei fraa*—my wife— and I...we...wanted to please *Der Herr*. Not that it was easy."

"How long did you date?"

"A year and a half."

"That is a long time to wait. I don't know how you did it." She swallowed. "So, do you think Josiah would have *married* me if he'd found out I was pregnant?"

*Ach*, the *Englisch* spoke so freely about such private matters. But it didn't even seem to faze Kayla. "I think he probably would. He was not perfect, but he was honorable in most respects. Even though it would've been a difficult decision and would have caused strife in his family, *jah*, I do think he would have become *Englisch* to marry you and raise his *dochder*."

"My heart hurts." Tears welled in her eyes once again. "We could have had a good life together. A happy family."

He shrugged, not knowing what to say. "What will you do now?"

"I don't know. I hadn't thought that far. Now that I know there is no possibility of rekindling a relationship with Bailey's father or even meeting him, I need to rethink my plan. Here I am, out in the middle of nowhere. I don't have any friends, not that I had a ton of close relationships in California. I don't even know anyone. Except you. I'm not sure where to go now."

He nodded. "That is why I called Dan Yoder. You arc already here. You could stay until you figure out what to do."

"I appreciate that, Silas. You're a very thoughtful man."

He stood from the couch. "I'm going to make coffee. Would you like some?"

She smiled. "No, thank you. If I have coffee now, I

might not be able to sleep. I think I'll just turn in."

Silas watched as Kayla walked to the bedroom she'd been sleeping in. If she did decide to stay and rent the Yoders' place, he'd eventually have to let Dan Yoder know that it wasn't actually him renting the place. He hadn't said that it was him, but he knew that's what Dan was most likely thinking when he'd asked. He wasn't quite sure whether he'd approve of a single *Englisch* mother staying in the empty house Silas was supposed to be caring for. And he definitely wouldn't approve of the two of them staying under the same roof—under *any* circumstances.

*Ach*, he'd gotten himself in a bad place. If any of the *g'may* ever found out that he was sharing a home with a woman, he'd be in deep trouble. No doubt he'd receive a visit from the deacon. He could only imagine the gossip.

But if it truly was *Der Herr* that caused Kayla and Bailey to turn in here, and if it was *Gott* who prompted him to come check the gutters and caused the creek to rise too high to cross over, then it did indeed seem like His will that Silas be here. Of course, it wasn't necessarily *Gott's* will that he sleep inside the house. But then, Kayla had said that she and Bailey would leave if he didn't. And the thought of the two of them being out in this weather and getting stranded on the side of the road or washed away in a flash flood was too much of a burden to take upon his shoulders. And now that he knew beyond the shadow of a doubt that Bailey was Josiah's *dochder*, he had a duty to make sure they were safe and provided for. It was a responsibility he'd gladly take on for his best friend, a way to honor him.

# SEVEN

Kayla had to get away from Silas, lest she become a blubbering, teary-eyed mess. Josiah was gone? No, it couldn't be so.

She could hardly believe she'd never see him again. She'd never stare into his eyes. She'd never be held in his arms. All hopes and dreams and fantasies about possibly creating a life together vanished. She'd thought he might be the one. The one to cure the sadness and grief she'd experienced since her parents' death. The one to cure her loneliness and give her and Bailey a steady home. But that would never be now.

She quickly peeked in on Bailey, who slept soundly in her temporary bed. Her daughter would never get a chance to meet her biological father. Would she forever carry around that longing? It all seemed so unfair. Why had God—if there was one—allowed them to come halfway across the country only to discover such heartbreaking news? It seemed cruel. Uncaring. Unloving.

What would they do now? Where would they go? She didn't have any answers. She was lost. Lost and completely alone. Oh, to have Mom or Dad here to ask advice from.

After Silas poured his coffee and sat at the table by himself, lost in thought, he opened the Bible he kept here. Since the Yoders had moved, this had been a sanctuary of sorts for him. A place to ponder. A place to deal with all he'd lost. A place to hope. A place to dream again.

He bowed his head. *Gott, help me to be like You. I want to do Your will. Please show me what it is. Show me the path You'd like me to walk in. Amen.*

He proceeded to read where he'd last left off in the book of Psalms. He read to verses five and six, then stopped. *Whoa.* He went back and read the verses again. *A father of the fatherless, and a judge of widows, is God in his holy habitation. God setteth the solitary in families...*

"Wow, *Gott*," he whispered. "Are You...? What are You trying to tell me?" He thought on the words he'd just prayed...*Help me to be like You.* "Do you want *me* to be a father to Josiah's child? Do you want me to step into his boots?"

He frowned. How could he possibly do that when Bailey and her mother were *Englisch*? *Show me how, Lord.*

He set the thought aside, and read through the remainder of the chapter. He let his eyes rest on the verses that had jumped out at him once again. *How, Gott?* He hadn't really expected an audible answer. He knew that *Der Herr* would answer in His own time.

He closed the Bible, rinsed out his coffee mug, and turned down the lantern's wick. Earlier, he'd brought in the extra one, the one he kept in the barn, so each of the adults would have a light. Kayla had the other one with her. He'd be able to see and feel his way to the bathroom, then to his upstairs bedroom in the dark. He had a feeling he wouldn't be getting much sleep tonight.

He walked past Kayla's room extra quietly, in case she was already asleep. It had been about thirty minutes since she'd gone to her bedroom, so it was a possibility. He stopped just a couple of steps past her door. He listened closely. The unmistakable sound of weeping caused his heart to clench tightly. He stopped. Should he just leave her be and allow her to grieve alone? *Bear ye one another's burdens...* He turned back and gently knocked on the door.

"Kayla, are you all right?" he spoke softly into the space between the door and the frame. He wasn't sure if the little one was a light sleeper or not, and he didn't wish to interrupt her rest. Seeing her mother in such a state would certainly be upsetting to the child.

Kayla sniffled but didn't answer.

*Ach, Gott.*

"May I come in?"

He thought he'd heard a faint affirmative answer.

He turned the knob and cautiously walked in. His eyes attempted to make out the interior of the bedroom. He quickly found the lantern on the nightstand and lit it. He'd expected to find Kayla sitting on the bed, but she was not. He didn't see her at all but heard her soft whimper. He walked around the bed and found her crumpled on the floor, her face buried in her hands. He knelt down next to her and pulled her close. "*Kumm.* It's okay."

She wrapped her arms around him and held him fiercely, releasing a barrage of tears on his shoulder.

*Ach,* he hated that she was hurting, mourning Josiah's death and the life they'd missed together, no doubt. *Why did he have to die, Lord?* He rubbed Kayla's back and sat with her for several minutes. He didn't speak, but simply held her, allowing her to cry.

She would speak when she was ready. *If* she trusted him enough to share.

After another ten minutes, she pulled away, and apologized.

"*Nee*, don't. You hurt much. You have nothing to be sorry for." He thought of telling her the verse about *Gott* keeping our tears in a bottle, but somehow, he didn't feel the timing was right. She was most likely still angry with *Gott*—maybe now more than ever. Perhaps he could help her move past that.

"I feel cheated. I feel like Bailey was cheated out of the life she could have had. It just isn't fair, Silas."

What could he say to that? In one aspect, he agreed. But in another, he knew that *Gott* was in control and that He could be trusted. He knew that *Der Herr* looked beyond our thoughts and feelings and instead saw our needs. *Gott* saw his needs. He saw Kayla's needs. And He saw Bailey's needs. And *Der Herr* would meet those needs in His perfect timing, in His perfect way. So, instead of speaking, he just nodded and listened to Kayla pour out her heart.

"I have no idea what to do now. I have no family. Bailey has no family." She forced away a tear.

"*Nee*, she has you."

"For now. But what if something were to happen to me, Silas? What if we get caught up in another storm, and she's left without a mother?"

"*Ach*, you have too many cares. You are still alive. *Gott* willing, nothing will happen to you." He attempted to sound confident.

"You don't know that. Were you expecting Josiah to die? Were you expecting to lose your wife and baby?"

"*Nee*, I was not." He released a long breath, reached for her hand, and looked into her eyes, willing her to absorb his confidence. "This storm will pass. I know it is hard to believe right now while you are in the middle of it, but it *will* pass. The sun will come out and shine again."

"I wish I had your assurance, your strength."

If she only knew that all his strength came from *Der Herr*. He had none on his own. *Gott* was everything to Him. His reason for rising up in the morning. His strength for each and every day. His entire reason for living. His hope. If he didn't have *Der Herr*, he would have nothing. But how could he portray that to someone who stood against *Gott*? He couldn't.

A verse came to his mind at that moment. *By this shall all men know that ye are my disciples, if ye have love one to another.* He closed his eyes and prayed silently. *Help me to show Kayla and Bailey Your love, Gott. Amen.*

She took a deep breath, and followed it with a yawn.

"*Ach*, you are tired. You should get some sleep." He began to rise, but Kayla stopped him.

"Wait." She leaned over and planted a feathery soft kiss on his cheek. "Thank you, Silas, for everything."

His face warmed at her nearness. *Ach*, this beautiful woman, who should've been his best friend's *fraa*, had just given him a kiss. And she was *Englisch*. *Englisch*, but *Gott* help him, he was developing feelings for her. He couldn't let himself be carried away. She was one hundred percent *verboten*. He needed to get out of there, to flee temptation.

He forced himself to rise, and exited her room. After he closed the door, he squeezed his eyes shut. *Please help her, Lord. Help her to see that You are not the enemy. Help her to find healing. Bless her and her dochder, Gott. And give me the strength to stay devoted to You and keep my thoughts pure. Amen.*

# EIGHT

Silas soaked in the sun's rays as they peaked over the eastern horizon. Perhaps the storms were finally passing them by. The weatherman had said to expect rain all week, but weathermen were often wrong. Only *Der Herr* knew the real forecast. The others simply made educated guesses.

He hoped Kayla had gotten a good night's sleep. He'd stayed awake another hour conversing with *Gott* after leaving Kayla's room. To tell the truth, it had felt *gut* to hold a woman in his arms once again. But he wouldn't allow his thoughts to go in that direction. He wasn't her husband. He didn't own that right.

Even so, he couldn't help but imagine what a life with Kayla and Bailey would look like. It didn't even seem like a viable option, yet he'd reasoned it out in his head many times last night. They were all alone. They needed him. And truth be told, he needed them too.

*Ach*, these were absurd thoughts considering he'd only known them a couple days.

There would be many hurdles to overcome if that scenario were to ever play out. Either he would need to jump the fence into the *Englisch* world—which he had *no* desire to do—or Josiah's *dochder* and Kayla could become Amish. He definitely preferred the latter. Because, even if he *wanted* to become *Englisch*, he would be shunned from his community. He simply couldn't imagine not being able to have fellowship with *Mamm* and *Daed* and all his siblings.

On the other hand, he was unsure if their community's *Ordnung* even allowed *Englischers* to join their church district. He'd never known anyone who had. And if their community disallowed it, he'd have no choice but to jump the fence if he wanted to be part of their family. But even if they did consent, she certainly wouldn't agree to the *Dordrecht Confession of Faith*. *Ach*, this was no easy thing for sure and for certain.

One thing he did know, though. He wanted Kayla and Bailey to meet his family. Bailey would get along wonderfully with his six-year-old sister, Emily. And he was certain that his sister Martha and *Mamm* would take a liking to Kayla. They'd have a lot of questions, no doubt, but Silas planned to explain the situation beforehand.

If the flood water had receded enough, he'd go home today. Sleeping in the same house with Kayla was not a *gut* idea. He needed to guard his thoughts and actions and to keep his heart with all diligence, as the Bible advised.

Kayla poured coffee into the mug as soon as she heard Silas stomping his boots outside the door. She was happy that she'd woken up early to make breakfast for the three of them, although Bailey still slept.

She thought of the night before. It had been rough, to say the least. First, she'd been in shock that Silas knew Josiah. Then, to hear of Josiah's death so soon after they'd parted ways—it had been devastating.

Even though she thought he might have been married and possibly had a family, she'd held out hope that he would still be single and available. She'd hoped he had a good reason for not contacting her. That, somehow, deep in his heart he still loved her. Apparently, he had. He hadn't been the jerk she'd chalked him up to be.

But every single hope she'd had vanished the instant Silas delivered the horrifying news. Every different scenario of their reunion. Every plan for their possible future. Gone. In a split second.

And then...*Silas*.

*Wow*. This man was amazing. If there was such a thing as a perfect gentleman, he'd definitely be in the running.

She could see Josiah and Silas being close friends, but it would seem that Silas had a leg up when it came to integrity. Of course, who was she to talk about integrity? She'd conceived a child out-of-wedlock, which, in this day and age, was nothing out of the ordinary. But she had a suspicion that for the Amish, it was a big thing.

"Mm...I smell coffee." Silas's cheery greeting pulled her out of her musings.

"Are you ready for some? I just poured you a cup." She set the mug on the small table.

"More than ready." He held the cup under his nose, closed his eyes, and inhaled.

She chuckled. "I do the same thing."

He took a drink. "It's *gut*."

"Your eggs are ready." She set the plate down in front of him, which also held a slice of bread.

He nodded. "*Denki*." He eyed her. "Did you eat already?"

"No."

He pushed the plate toward her. "You eat first." And there was that thoughtfulness again.

"Oh, no. I made those for you. I'll wait for Bailey."

He frowned, looking like he might argue, but instead shrugged, bowed his head momentarily, then took a bite.

"Sun is shining today," he remarked.

She took the other seat. "I know. I'm still trying to figure out what to do."

"Would you like to meet my family? If the creek has gone down, I plan to go home today."

"Oh." For some reason, she felt disappointed Silas would no longer be there. "Yeah, we could meet them."

"I'll see if *Mamm* would like to have you over for supper tonight. You wouldn't mind a home-cooked meal, would you?"

"It would beat eating eggs for every meal. Not that I'm complaining."

His smile was easy. "I'm getting a little tired of them too."

"I wanted to say thank you again for last night. That was sweet."

He nodded once, obviously uncomfortable. "I'd like to help you any way I can."

She reached over and cupped her hand over his. Did he feel a connection between them too? Like something in their world had shifted last night in the bedroom? "I really appreciate that."

He didn't take his hand away, but cleared his throat slightly. "The little one is still asleep?"

"Yes." She reluctantly removed her hand. Perhaps the feeling was one-sided.

"She will like my sister Emily."

"You have a sister?"

"*Jah*. Several."

"How old is Emily?"

"Six."

"Oh, good. Yes, I'm sure they will become fast friends. Bailey loves meeting new children. She gets along easily with others."

He nodded. "I'll take a ride down the road after breakfast. If the road is decent, I'll come back to get you and Bailey for supper. If *Mamm* didn't make other plans."

"Just in case, what time do you think that will be so we're sure to be ready?"

"I'm thinking four thirty. *Daed* usually gets home from work about five. I suspect he worked today now that the roadways are probably draining."

"Speaking of work, do you have a job you should be at? Not that it's any of my business."

"*Nee*, it's fine. *Jah*, I work with *Daed* on construction projects and I also work around the farm. On rainy days, there's only so much work that can be done outside. *Daed* will not be missing me."

She nodded. "That suits you."

Construction. She should have guessed. That would explain the well-defined chest she'd seen in the basement and his muscular frame. She grinned at the thought of his arms around her last night. She wouldn't mind a repeat of that nearness—without her sobbing on his shoulder. "Okay. We'll be ready by four thirty then."

Silas sipped the last of his coffee and rinsed out the mug.

He'd been mulling over the best course of action concerning Kayla and Bailey. Should he inform Josiah's family of the situation? He didn't feel right not letting his friend's folks know that they had a grandchild.

"How do you feel about contacting Josiah's family?"

Her eyes widened. "Oh. I guess I hadn't thought of that. Do you...how do you think they would respond?"

"I don't know. But if Bailey is their *grossboppli*, I'm thinking they'll want to know."

"I haven't mentioned anything to Bailey. I'm still trying to figure out what to tell her."

"What does she know?"

"She just knows that her daddy lives somewhere far

away. I'm sure she must have dreams of meeting him." She swallowed and brushed away a tear. "I don't know what to tell her. I don't want to break her heart."

*Ach.* "I imagine it would be a difficult thing for a child. But the truth is usually best."

He ached to tell her his thoughts for the possible future, but it was too soon. How would Bailey feel if Silas stepped into her daddy's shoes? Would she be pleased? Would Kayla even allow it?

He should probably seek advice from *Mamm* and *Daed* and the leaders. But what if they were against it? He didn't even want to entertain that thought, but it was likely to be the case. Kayla and Bailey were *Englisch,* and he was not. He was a baptized member of the Amish church, which meant his future in the Plain community was set. There would be no breaking of his vows to the church. There would be no jumping the fence.

*Jah,* there was much to think and pray about. Perhaps he'd drive out to bishop Jerry Bontrager's place after he stopped off at home.

He eyed Kayla before donning his hat. "Would you like me to contact Josiah's family?"

She nodded. "Yeah. Sure."

"I'll call Pennsylvania today then." The thought both comforted and worried him. How would

Josiah's family respond? Would they be accepting of Kayla and Bailey? Would they want them to live nearby? If so, that would mean Kayla and Bailey would move far away. He wasn't sure he liked that idea. The thought of having his own family again had grown on him. It would be difficult to see the two of them go, for sure and certain.

"Silas, wait." He turned back around at Kayla's voice. "What should I wear to your parents' house tonight?"

He lifted his eyebrows and smiled. "Clothes."

He winked, then stepped out the door.

# NINE

Kayla stood open-mouthed as Silas sauntered to his buggy. Had he just *flirted* with her?

She couldn't be certain, but she was pretty sure that single word held more than one meaning. Clothes, indeed. She smiled, shaking her head. She guessed *he* wouldn't be forgetting the first time they'd met anytime soon either. Of course, she didn't imagine he would. It's not every day a man unintentionally bursts in on a woman changing her clothes. Probably even less so in his culture.

"What a way to make a first impression, Kayla," she mumbled to herself.

Silas was glad to see that the water had receded enough to safely pass over. He thought about everything that had happened in the two days since he'd crossed through the raging creek. Finding Kayla and Bailey in the Yoders' home had been a surprise, to say the least. And then to find out they were kin to his best friend, well, it almost seemed like *Der Herr* had specially delivered them straight to him all wrapped up with a beautiful red bow. It almost seemed like *Gott* had given him a brand-new family to love, since He'd taken away his first one. It almost seemed like *he* had been sent to *them* as well. Why else would all the pieces fit together so perfectly? It *had* to be the work of *Der Herr*, didn't it?

But he shouldn't get ahead of himself. Just because things seemed one way didn't necessarily mean that it was ordained by *Gott*. After all, Kayla and Bailey were *Englisch*. He needed to keep reminding himself of that fact. Because no matter how much he longed to have another family, one with Josiah's widow and *dochder* was not likely. Not that she was his widow indeed, but that was how Silas considered her. Because he was sure his friend would have left everything to be with her and their *boppli*. If *he* were in that situation, he would've married Kayla. Of that, he was sure and certain.

*Ach*, he'd been so lost in thought, he hadn't even realized Strider had pulled into his driveway. He really should pay more attention to the road. Because the last thing Kayla needed in her life was another senseless tragedy. How could he be so careless? *Dummkopp*, he chided himself.

He pulled Strider up to the hitching post, freed him from his constraints, then led him to an empty stall and gave him fresh oats. If the ground hadn't been so wet, he would've turned him out into the pasture. With the muddy ground, he didn't want to chance an injured ankle. That had happened once before, and it had proven to be costly.

"You finally showed up. It's about time, *bruder*," his brother commented. Silas looked up at his seventeen-year-old brother, Paul, who was currently mucking out a stall. "We thought you drowned. *Mamm* had in mind to send out a search party until *Daed* suggested we check the phone shanty first."

Silas grunted. He could only imagine his family's reaction if they happened upon him and Kayla alone in the house together. "He probably wouldn't have been able to make it through the creek. Me and Strider barely made it through."

"That was some storm. *Daed* thought we might be getting a tornado too."

He'd definitely experienced a tornado, but not the kind Paul was thinking of. It was amazing how the trajectory of a life could change in just a couple of days. He hadn't even known about Kayla and Bailey at the beginning of the week, but now? It seemed like his every thought revolved around them.

"Hello? Silas?" His brother's hand waved in front of his face.

He shook his head.

"Are you okay, *bruder*? You seem a little preoccupied."

Indeed. "*Jah*, I'm fine. Just a lot on my mind right now."

His brother frowned. "Wanna talk about it?"

*Ach*, now his brother believed he was missing his *fraa*. "*Nee*." He'd soon find out anyhow.

Silas left the barn and headed toward the *dawdi haus*. He'd occupied the solitary dwelling since he and his *fraa* married. Since his *grosseldre* still lived in Pennsylvania, his folks allowed him to use it even after his wife's death. If *Mammi* and *Dawdi* were to ever move to Indiana, however, he'd have to give up his home to accommodate his grandparents. If that ever happened, he hoped to have enough income to purchase the Yoders' property.

And he yearned for it now more than ever. After spending time there with Kayla and Bailey, he imagined the three of them living in that home as a family. It would be perfect. Bailey could go to school with his sister, Emily. He and Kayla could run the little store out front. And he'd have the property to care for. If they needed more income, he could always work on the construction crew with John Stoltzfus and *Daed*.

*Ach*, there he went again dreaming of something that would most likely never come to fruition. Chances were, Josiah's folks would want their *grossboppli* close to them. Which meant Kayla and Bailey would move to Pennsylvania. Far away from him in Indiana. A world away by horse and buggy.

He now walked through the adjoining door that connected his small *dawdi haus* to his folks' main dwelling. As usual, *Mamm's* kitchen smelled like fresh baked dessert.

"*Mei sohn* has returned." *Mamm* smiled, pulling muffins out of the oven, as if on cue.

"Mm...what kind are those?"

"Apple. Your favorite. I made blueberry earlier."

Wouldn't Kayla and Bailey love to have some? No doubt, after eating nothing but eggs.

"Something on your mind?"

*Ach*, he was way too easy to read, it seemed. "*Jah*. I need to talk to you and *Daed* about something. And Jerry Bontrager."

*That* had gotten *Mamm's* attention. "You need to speak with the bishop? Sounds serious." She sat down on one of the kitchen chairs and motioned Silas to do the same.

He glanced around. "Where are the others?"

"The little ones are at school. Paul is out doing chores. Martha and Susan are cutting out dresses upstairs. It is just us."

He nodded. "I had a surprise when I went to Yoders'. There was an *Englisch* woman there in the house with her *dochder*."

*Mamm's* eyes flew wide. "A trespasser? In Dan Yoder's house?"

He'd never considered Kayla and Bailey trespassers, but he supposed that might be the proper word for the interlopers. He'd just considered them strangers in need of protection from the elements. But he quickly discovered they were much more than that, they'd been sent to him from *Der Herr*. The more he thought on it, the more convinced he became.

He explained. "They were looking for shelter from the storm and the little one needed a bathroom."

She offered a hesitant nod, not quite certain where this conversation was going.

"I discovered they are kin to Josiah."

"Josiah? But he is *dot*."

"Bailey, the *maedel*, is his *dochder*."

*Mamm* covered her open mouth. "Josiah was...? He had a family?"

"He died before he could learn about the *boppli*."

"Do his folks know?"

"*Nee*. I plan to call them today." He shook his head. "It's like *Der Herr* sent Kayla and Bailey here. They were on their way to Pennsylvania."

"It seems so." *Mamm* frowned. "But they are *Englischers*, you say?"

"*Jah*."

"How long have they been there?"

"Just two days, I think. They turned in when the storm was so bad. The roads were flooded."

"And they slept in the Yoders' *haus*?"

"*Jah*." He dreaded the question he knew *Mamm* would ask next.

"And you? You did not sleep in the *haus* too."

"It has seven bedrooms." He grimaced.

"*Ach*, Silas."

"We didn't do anything, *Mamm*." His face burned. That wasn't a lie, was it?

"You know that is not the point. It looks bad. Very bad. And you are setting a bad example."

"I would have come back home, but the flood water was too high."

"You should have slept in the barn then." She was right, of course. "What will happen when the leaders find out?"

"I didn't plan on telling them."

"You know things like this have a way of getting out. Silas, something like this is scandalous. You're putting your reputation at risk."

He'd have to make sure to tell Kayla not to mention the way they'd met. If *Mamm* thought the situation was scandalous now, he could only imagine what she'd think if she knew all the details. But still, they hadn't done anything inappropriate. No matter how inappropriate it may have looked.

"Just think about this, Silas. You spent two nights *alone* in the same home as an *Englisch* woman. In the minister's home, no less!"

"I told you we didn't do anything, *Mamm*." His frustration mounted, mostly because *Mamm* was right and he knew it.

"*Ach*, Silas. You know better."

He hated that tone.

"You will most likely need to make a confession before the leaders."

"I can do that."

"There's a good chance you won't be able to care for Dan Yoder's place anymore."

"What?"

"If this *Englisch* woman is found in the *familye* way, Dan Yoder will feel responsible for allowing sin on his property."

*Ach*, did *Mamm* not believe what he'd just told her? "*Mamm*, you know me. You know I wouldn't do that."

"You are a man, Silas. And man is capable of much sin. She was apparently able to sway Josiah."

He couldn't believe what *Mamm* was insinuating. Yes, he was a man. Yes, he was capable of sin. But that didn't mean he *had* sinned with Kayla. And he resented that *Mamm* seemed to have him tried and convicted when he was truly innocent. And it wasn't fair to judge Kayla either. Just because she'd made a mistake with Josiah didn't mean she was a harlot, for goodness' sake. But he wouldn't disrespect *Mamm* by arguing with her.

He sighed. "I invited them over for supper tonight. I hope that is all right."

"I will set two extra plates."

Perhaps he shouldn't have even mentioned anything to his family and just sent Kayla and Bailey on their way to Pennsylvania with the address to Josiah's folks' place. Then no one would have known.

But that hadn't seemed like the right thing to do. He felt like they were his personal responsibility now. And what of the Scriptures he'd read? Could that have been just a coincidence that he would read those words on the exact day he'd found out about Josiah's family? He'd thought not. He hadn't imagined the words he'd read. It was as though *Der Herr* had spoken directly to him.

If *Mamm* had any idea what he was thinking right now, she'd likely have a fit. Well, he wouldn't tell her. At least, not yet.

He needed to speak with the bishop. But after *Mamm's* reaction, he was hesitant now. Perhaps it would be better to just lie low for the time being. Now that he was back at home, there would be no cause for anyone to suspect anything.

He knew what he would *not* do though. He would not cast off Kayla and Bailey just because they were *Englisch*. And he would not assume the worst of Kayla because she had a past. Hadn't every person alive done things they weren't proud of?

He admitted that he didn't know Kayla all that well, but he could tell a few things. She was a *gut mamm*. She was protective and responsible and cared for her *dochder's* needs. And she seemed selfless, and considerate, and kind.

No, she didn't have a *gut* relationship with *Gott*. That was one negative thing, for sure and certain. But that was only because she was hurting. She didn't understand that *Der Herr* was the one who healed broken hearts, not the one who broke them. Silas desired to help her see who *Gott* really was. He was the lover of her soul. The one who'd given everything to show her that He loved her, that He cares for her.

*Open her eyes to Your love, Gott.*

# TEN

Silas couldn't quell the spring in his step. Despite his mother's reaction, he was excited to bring Kayla and Bailey home. He was confident she'd change her mind once she spent a little time getting to know Kayla. At least, he hoped so.

His brother whistled as Silas exited the bathroom. "Woo, *bruder*." Paul's brow shot up. "If I didn't know any better, I'd think you were going courtin'."

"I am not."

"You don't even look like that for meeting." Paul challenged.

"I do too."

His brother crossed his arms over his chest and smirked. "Cologne?"

He shrugged in nonchalance. "I just took a shower. I don't want to smell bad."

"Courting." His brother nodded. "I'm surprised you didn't shave too."

"Widowers don't shave." Silas shook his head. Was he courting? Not in a literal sense. But if he could... *Jah*, if Kayla was Amish, he'd definitely be courting her. But she wasn't. So he wasn't.

Silas frowned. "She's *Englisch*."

"Uh-huh."

As soon as Kayla stepped out of the house, Silas's heart did a little flip. She wore a short white floral dress that hit just above her knee, matching white sandals, and just a bit of makeup. *Ach*, she was a beautiful woman.

Bailey wore an identical outfit, but with no makeup. Did *Englischers* usually put face paint on their *kinner*? He couldn't be sure.

He stepped down from the buggy to help the two of them onto the back seat. He was a little disappointed not to have Kayla by his side, but it was probably better this way. He doubted either Kayla or Bailey had ever ridden in a buggy. He planned to take it easy with Strider so he could spend as much time with the two of them as possible.

"You look very handsome, Silas," Kayla smiled.

He nodded, unsure of how to respond. It wasn't their way to heap on compliments.

"I hope Bailey and I are dressed appropriately to meet your family. I was unsure of what to wear but I figured a dress would be best."

"It's fine." He smiled. "I hope you are hungry."

Kayla fidgeted as Silas drove them to his family's home. He'd been mostly quiet, and she wondered if he was nervous about bringing them home. She knew that *she* was nervous.

Bailey, on the other hand, bounced on the plush buggy seat remarking about each and every thing they passed. She was super excited to meet Silas's sister. It would be wonderful if her daughter could make a friend. If they ended up staying in this area, she would need friends her age.

Kayla wondered what a future here in Indiana would look like. Was there a school nearby that Bailey could attend once the school year began again? Would they have regular contact with Silas and his family? He had said that he was taking care of the property where they'd stayed the last couple nights. She wondered how often he stopped by there.

Just the thought of him not being there, now that the

road was clear, brought a touch of sadness. She enjoyed having a man in the house. Bailey had taken to Silas like gum on a horseshoe. She adored him. And he seemed to be inching his way into Kayla's heart as well. No, not inching, more like catapulting. She hadn't known many men like him. He was a rare breed indeed.

Now that she had no chance of rekindling a romantic relationship with Josiah, perhaps she would consider opening her heart to someone else. She hadn't dated at all. As a matter of fact, Bailey's father had been the first boy she'd ever kissed. And she'd fallen head over heels for him. When he never contacted her, she'd thought he'd just used her, broken her heart. She didn't know if the reality of the situation was better or worse. She supposed it was a little bit of both. She was glad that to know Josiah had loved her, as he'd declared. But sad that Bailey would never know her father.

"You're quiet back there." Silas's voice pulled her out of her musings.

"Just thinking."

He nodded, then maneuvered the horse and buggy into a driveway. "Well, here we are. Are you two ready to meet my family?"

"Ready as we can be, I guess." Butterflies still flittered about in her stomach.

Bailey bounced on the seat. "I'm ready to meet my new friend!"

Kayla and Silas shared a smile.

"I'm sure Emily is excited to meet you too. As soon as I unhitch Strider, I'll take you inside to meet her."

"*Denki*, Mr. Silas." All her teeth showed in her smile. Well, except for the missing one in front. Her "Mister Silas" sounded more like "Mithter Thilath."

Well, this was it. For better or for worse, she would be meeting Silas's family. She blew out a breath as her stomach turned over. At least Silas would be at her side.

Silas made quick work of releasing Strider, then led the way to the house. *Mamm*, Martha, and Susan were busy finishing up the meal preparation, while Emily helped out by setting the table.

"*Mamm*, Martha, Susan, Emily, this is Kayla and her *dochder*, Bailey," Silas introduced.

"Hello, it's *gut* to meet you. Silas tells us that Bailey is—"

"Uh, *Mamm*!" He abruptly shook his head. "*Jah*, Bailey is five. Just a year younger than Emily."

His mother frowned.

"She doesn't know about her father," Silas said the

words in Pennsylvania Dutch so Bailey wouldn't understand.

"Mr. Silas taught me some Amish words too!" Bailey beamed.

"Well, Emily is learning English in school, so maybe you can teach each other," Silas suggested. "Emily, why don't you go show Bailey your room? If it's all right with her *mudder*?"

Kayla nodded. "Yes, that's fine with me, if Bailey's comfortable."

"I'm fine, Mommy." Bailey latched on to Emily's hand and smiled. "I'm ready."

The adults grinned as the two young girls disappeared in short order.

"I didn't realize that Amish children didn't speak English," Kayla commented.

"They can understand most of it. They learn to speak it more once they start school. Pennsylvania Dutch, what we call Amish, is spoken in the home, then they'll learn English and a little German in school," Martha explained.

"May I help with dinner?" Kayla offered.

"Sure. You may set this on the table." His mother handed Kayla a pitcher of lemonade. "Silas, will you call in your brother and father?"

"Sure." He nodded to Kayla to be sure she could

handle being amongst the womenfolk, then went to do his mother's bidding.

A couple of minutes later, the men entered the house.

Paul hung back and stared at their guest. "*Schee, bruder*. No wonder you got all dressed up and put cologne on. *Ach*, Josiah had good taste," he half-whispered in Silas's ear.

"Shh…" He elbowed his brother. "*Kumm*, supper is ready. Don't embarrass me."

"*Ach*, now would I do that?" Paul's eyes sparkled with mischief.

Silas shook his head. He'd be holding his breath the entire time they sat at the table.

# ELEVEN

Silas sighed once the meal was finished. Somehow, unbeknownst to him, Paul—and everybody else, for that matter—managed not to embarrass him or Kayla during supper. Wonders never ceased!

Kayla currently helped wash dishes, conversing with *Mamm* and his *schweschdern*. They seemed to be getting along great so far. Emily and Bailey went straight back to Emily's room to play immediately after supper had finished. He had a feeling Kayla might have a hard time talking her into leaving tonight.

As soon as Kayla finished up in the kitchen, Silas hoped to whisk her away on a walk around their property. They needed to be alone so he could tell her how his phone conversation with Josiah's folks went. He'd planned to talk to Jerry Bontrager too, but there hadn't been enough hours in the day. Perhaps he'd take a ride out to the bishop's place tomorrow instead.

He currently waited in the family room. His father read *The Budget*, while he and Paul indulged in a game of checkers. He'd been lost in thought, not paying much mind to the game at hand.

"Crown me." Paul grinned.

"What?" Silas blinked, then stared down at the board. "I didn't even see that."

"Seems like you're not seeing much of anything these days...well, maybe *one* thing." His brother glanced toward the kitchen where the women worked, then shot him an accusing look. "So, what's going on between you two?"

Silas frowned. "Going on? Nothing."

"Right."

Silas shook his head.

Paul leaned in close and whispered, "According to *Mamm*, you and Kayla spent two nights together. Alone. In the same house." Paul's brow lifted.

"She told you that?" He'd never known his mother to be a gossip.

"*Nee*. I was eavesdropping on her conversation with *Daed*." He winked.

"*Ach*, Paul."

"Well?"

"It was innocent. Nothing happened."

"Have you seen the way she looks at you? Why on earth not?"

Silas frowned at his brother. "Because I'm not that type of man. And I'm not in *rumspringa* anymore." He pointed his finger at Paul's chest. "And *you* shouldn't be that type of man either."

"Tell me you didn't do anything like that in *rumspringa*." He challenged.

"I didn't do anything like that in *rumspringa*."

"Uh-huh." Paul's brow shot up. "And *Josiah* was your best friend?"

Silas crossed his arms over his chest. "This conversation is over, and so is the game." He abruptly folded the game, sending all the red and black checkers to the middle of the board before his brother could protest.

"What'd you do that for? I was winning."

"Okay, so you won. Game over."

"You're testy when you're in love." Paul prodded. "I want a rematch."

"Another time, *bruder*. And I'm not in love." He growled, frustrated with his brother's careless words.

"Mm...hm."

Silas stood as the women walked into the room. His gaze couldn't help but single out a certain somebody. Okay, so maybe he was attracted to Kayla.

"Kayla, would you like to see our farm?" He grinned like a fool. He knew his brother was staring at the exchange, but he ignored him.

"Sure. Let me just check on Bailey."

"I'll show you where they are," Martha offered.

Silas stared after Kayla as she walked out of the room toward Emily's bedroom.

"Martha will go with you," *Mamm* stated.

Silas turned and looked at his mother. "*Nee.* I want to speak with her alone. There are things we need to discuss."

Paul came up behind Silas and slapped his shoulder blade. "Alone, huh? You're doomed." He laughed, then continued on outside.

"You can watch us from a distance if you're worried about anything happening." Silas told his mother. "We're adults, *Mamm*."

"Leave them be," his father finally spoke up. "Silas is a *gut* boy. He knows how to behave himself."

"Thank you, *Daed*." At least *someone* trusted him.

Kayla peeked into the room where Bailey and Emily sat playing on the floor.

Emily stood up and moved behind Bailey. She took

a hairbrush and started brushing Bailey's hair. "Okay, this might hurt a little bit. Try not to cry."

Kayla wondered if she should step in.

Emily parted Bailey's hair down the middle, then pulled it back tightly. "Does that hurt?"

"A little, but I'm okay." Bailey winced.

"I cry sometimes when *Mamm* does mine."

"I won't cry. I'm five now."

"Well, I'm six and I cry once in a while 'cause it hurts." Emily twisted Bailey's hair, then stuck a bunch of pins in to keep the bun in place. "Sorry, I think I poked you."

"That's okay."

"Does it feel tight? 'Cause it's supposed to feel tight."

"It does."

"*Gut.*"

"That's means good, right?"

"*Jah.*" Emily placed her prayer *kapp* on Bailey's head.

That was when Kayla noticed her daughter was also wearing an Amish dress. She had to get Silas and show him. She hurried to the other room.

"Silas," she whispered. "Come here. You have to see this."

He nodded, then followed her to Emily's room.

She put her index finger to her lips to signal silence. He nodded.

They both looked into the room.

"There. Now you're Amish just like me." Emily surveyed Bailey's attire. "And you can come to my school too. We'll be friends."

Kayla looked at Silas and they shared a smile. He'd been right about the girls getting along.

He motioned over his shoulder for her to follow him.

They walked back to the living room, then he finally spoke. "The girls look like they're having a good time."

"Yeah, they are." Perhaps it *had* been God who brought Silas and his family into their lives. This was beginning to seem like more than just coincidence. She pushed the thought away just as quickly as it had surfaced.

"You ready to take that walk now?"

"Sure. Let's go while the girls are occupied."

His mother said something to him in Pennsylvania Dutch that Kayla didn't understand.

He replied back in their language as well.

They stepped out the door.

"My mother said not to be too long because she will have dessert and coffee ready soon," Silas translated.

"Mm...sounds good."

Silas looked around. "My brother is probably spying on us somewhere."

"I get the feeling that your family isn't used to having non-Amish people over often." She glanced back at the house and noticed some of Silas's family members peeking out the side of the curtain. She giggled. "I think they're watching us."

"*Kumm*, let's go where they can't watch us." He cocked his head. "And, j*ah*. We do sometimes have *Englisch* folks over, it's just a different situation with you."

"How so?"

He led her to a wooded area. "Watch your step. It might be muddy."

She frowned at her sandals. Perhaps she should have thought a little more practically.

He continued. "Well, for one, you're an attractive, single young woman. Two, you have a child with no father present. And, three, we spent two nights together alone in the same house."

"Yeah, I guess that does sound bad from their standpoint." She smiled at Silas and lightly punched his arm. "You think I'm attractive?"

"*Ach*, very much so."

"Well, you're pretty hot yourself."

He chuckled and shook his head.

"You don't think so?" She smiled.

"I think *Englischers* speak too freely."

"Well, it's the truth."

Silas cleared his throat. "I brought you out here to talk about Josiah's folks."

"Change of subject, huh? Okay, I'll take the bait. What about them?"

"They would like to meet their *grossdochder*."

Silas waited while she stepped over some branches that had fallen in the path. He took her hand to stable her, and his gentleness once again stirred her heart. She glanced up to see if the emotions she was feeling were one-sided. His eyes sparked with something dangerously akin to desire. Then he must've realized his hand still held hers, and dropped it. The moment had been broken, but she wouldn't be forgetting the look in his eyes anytime soon.

What were they talking about? Oh, yeah. "Bailey's grandparents. What should I do? Do you think I should make a trip out to Pennsylvania to meet them?"

"You said you were in need of money, ain't so?"

"In a way, yes. I do have money from my parents' life insurance policy, but I wanted to save that for Bailey's college. I'm trying to use as little as possible so she has a little nest egg."

"I see." He frowned.

"But I can still pay rent to Mr. Yoder."

He nodded. "Josiah's folks will likely come here."

"Oh. When?"

"They did not say. I'd suspect maybe on a holiday." He shook his head. "And I don't know how long Dan Yoder will want to rent out his place. He had planned to sell it."

"Oh."

"He thinks I am the one renting."

"Oh. Do you think he'd approve of me renting?"

"I can't say. I think not. But I might have a solution if he doesn't."

"What?" She laughed. "Marry me?"

Silas's eyes nearly jumped out of their sockets.

"I was joking, Silas. Take a deep breath."

His lips pressed together in a thin line. Had she offended him?

She backpedaled. "Not that we would be bad together. I just...it would be absurd, wouldn't it?"

"I am only allowed to marry an Amish woman."

Of course. "And I'm not Amish." She shook her head. "What solution were you talking about?"

"I could rent it and you and Bailey could stay in my folks' *dawdi haus*, where I live now." He shrugged. "I haven't discussed this with my folks, but they might agree."

"*Dawdi haus*?"

"Yes. It is a very small house attached to the main home. It's mostly used for grandparents, but mine are still in Pennsylvania with my aunts and uncles. So, when *mei fraa* and I got hitched, we moved in there."

"But if I move in there and Mr. Yoder plans to sell, where would you live?"

"*Ach*, I hope he'll sell it to me. But if not, I can move back into my old bedroom in the big house."

"Really? You want to buy that large farm?"

He stared out into the field as they came to a clearing. "I hope to have a family someday. I will most likely not be a widower forever, *Gott* willing."

Somehow, the thought of him being married to some Amish woman brought an inexplicable sadness.

"No, I wouldn't think so. A hot Amish guy like you." She winked, loving the color that crept up his neck.

"*Ach, Englischers.*"

# TWELVE

Silas dreaded dropping off Kayla and Bailey. He hated the fact that they'd be alone in the house. *Ach*, he wished he could stay too. But he couldn't. He'd already caused enough stir amongst his family. It wouldn't do if gossip started in the community.

"I had a good time with your family tonight, Silas. They seem like nice people," Kayla spoke from the seat behind him.

Bailey had leaned over and laid her head in her mother's lap. "Me too. Emily and me are best friends now."

"Emily and I, sweetheart."

"Emily and I. We're twins too. Mommy, can I be Amish like Emily?"

Silas's brow raised, curious how Kayla would respond.

"There's a lot more to being Amish than dressing like Emily, honey."

Jennifer Spredemann

"Like what?"

"Well, like they don't drive cars. They have to use a horse and buggy."

"All the time?" Her voice filled with wonder.

Silas chuckled. "Not all the time. Sometimes we pay *Englisch* people money to take us places if we have to go further than we want to take our buggies."

"Isn't that cheating?"

Silas laughed. "No. It's in our *Ordnung*."

"What's *Ordnung*?"

"It's a list of rules that our people follow. Every year, the leaders get together, and they decide if we want to keep things as they are or add new exceptions to the rules we have."

"I don't understand that." Bailey mumbled, obviously exhausted from her playtime.

"They're just rules their church follows, honey," Kayla explained.

The buggy turned quiet for a little while.

"I think she's out," Kayla whispered.

Silas turned the buggy into the Yoders' lane. "Just in time."

He guided the horse to the hitching post. "Wait there. I'll get her out."

He opened the sliding door and jumped down. "Hand her here."

He reached his arms out and gently took Bailey from Kayla's arms. This felt so natural. Like they were his family. But they weren't. And he needed to continue to remind himself of that fact.

Kayla dismounted the buggy as well. "I'll get the door."

Silas followed behind her. "I'll take her to her room. Do you need to awaken her to use the restroom?"

"I'll let her sleep for now, then wake her up to go before I go to bed."

"You plan to be up for a while?"

"Yeah. I think I'll have a cup of this tea your mother gave me. Please tell her thank you for everything again."

"Did you get your bread and muffins from the buggy?"

"Yeah. It will be nice to have it for breakfast in the morning. I think I might make a trip to the store tomorrow."

"Really? If you do, would you mind stopping by the house? *Mamm* or one of my sisters might want to go. If that's okay."

"That sounds like fun actually. They can show me where everything is."

He pointed to the south. "Madison is that way. You got Walmart and Aldi there." He pointed north. "Versailles is that way. Not much there, but they do have an IGA grocery store and a couple of dollar stores. Oh, and a few fast food restaurants and other places to eat. It's closer."

"Oh, that's good to know."

"They have a nice library too."

"Oh, I'm sure Bailey will love that." She smiled.

"Well, I should probably go, then."

Kayla frowned. "Already? You're welcome to stay and have some tea with me."

It did sound tempting. He shook his head. "*Mamm* will start to worry."

"Uh, about that. I feel like I should probably set her mind at ease." She shook her head. "Bailey's father was actually the first and only man I've ever kissed. I was sixteen. And then when I found out that I was pregnant, I was kind of scared to get too close to anybody. You know what I mean?"

Wow, that revelation had been a bit of a surprise. "My wife was the only woman that I kissed too."

"Really?"

"*Jah.*"

"I don't know if that will help as far as your mom is concerned."

He shrugged. "It might."

"I just don't want her to think that because I had a daughter out of wedlock that I sleep with every guy I meet."

"I'm sure she didn't think that." He allowed his eyes to sweep over her dress and take in her loveliness. That had been a mistake. "Maybe I'll stay a couple of minutes."

Ten extra minutes wouldn't hurt anybody, he reasoned. And she sounded like she wanted him to stay.

"I'll put the water on. Would you like to take a seat on the couch?"

"*Ach*, just a minute. I forgot something in the buggy." He jogged back out to retrieve the forgotten items.

He walked back into the house and waltzed to the kitchen. "Here, I brought these for you." He handed her the grocery bag.

She opened it and peered inside. "Oh, good." She pulled out a few plates, mugs, and utensils, along with a few other kitchen necessities. "Wow. Thank you, Silas. You're so thoughtful."

He wouldn't tell her those were the dishes he and his wife had used in their home. Somehow, that seemed too intimate. "Thought you and Bailey might want to eat at the same time."

She began putting the items away. "That's really nice."

He leaned back against the counter, admiring the

view. It almost felt like the three of them were a little family.

She stepped near, and her hand lightly caressed his cheek. "I don't know how to thank you for everything you've done."

His eyes locked with hers and a slight smile lifted at the corner of her mouth. *Ach.*

This woman was beautiful inside and out. He knew he shouldn't want her, that he shouldn't be having these feelings for an *Englischer*, but...

He leaned down and her eyes draped shut. His lips lowered to hers in a slow gentle kiss. If he could only hold on to this moment forever. Her hands pressed against his chest causing his muscles to tense, the warmth of her touch seeping through his shirt, sending a wave of desire through him. He moved his hands to cradle her face and his fingers wove through her silky hair that smelled like peaches or strawberries or some other sweet fruit. Her arms went around him, her soft form pressing into him. *Ach.*

He enjoyed every blissful second, wishing it would never have to end. But it needed to. Right now.

He forced himself away, his breath ragged.

"Silas." Kayla's eyes were dreamy. She pulled him close again, bringing his hand around her waist.

He shouldn't. He *really* shouldn't, but the

temptation was so strong and he was so weak. He didn't even want to fight it. *Gott*, help him.

His head seemed to lower of its own accord and his mouth once again found hers. He groaned with pleasure as warmth moved through every fiber of his being. "*Ach*, Kayla. Kayla." His hungry kisses traveled to her neck and collar bone. A soft gasp escaped her lips.

"Mommy?"

They jumped apart at Bailey's tiny voice. His crazy heartbeat refused to still.

"Wha-what is it, honey?" Kayla blew out a breath. She visibly trembled, her cheeks alive with color.

"Can Mr. Silas be my daddy?"

Kayla's eyes met his, and he saw as much desire in them as he felt in his own. "I...uh... Bailey, why aren't you asleep, honey?"

"I had to go potty and I was thirsty," she whined.

Kayla moved to fill a cup with just a couple ounces of water. "Here. Not too much. I don't want you to have an accident."

She took a sip of water. "Can Mr. Silas live here with us?"

"We'll talk about that later, okay? But right now, you need to get to sleep." She patted Bailey's bottom, sending her back to her room.

They listened for her door to close.

Silas pushed away from the counter. "I should go."

"Wait, Silas. We should talk. About the kiss."

The kiss? *Ach*, it was so much more than just a kiss. It was his hopes and dreams and desires all bundled up in a few powerful wonderful moments. Disguised as a kiss, maybe, but, oh, so much more.

"Can we make this work?" She pointed back and forth to each of them. "Us?"

He wished to *Gott* that they could. But she didn't even have faith in the *Gott* he'd devoted his life to. *Ach*, what had he been thinking? He hadn't. *Nee*, he'd been letting his fleshly desires rule his actions. And now he'd given Kayla false hope.

"I don't know." He shook his head.

"I'm serious, Silas. I've barely known you a couple of days, but I feel like I've known you all my life. You're so good with Bailey, and she adores you. I didn't come here expecting to find you, yet somehow you're here. It's almost like..."

"Like *Gott* brought us together?"

"I don't know, but it would almost seem that way. Honestly, I've thought more about the things of God in the last couple of days than in my past twenty-one years." His skin tingled as her fingers slowly trailed his forearm. "Bailey and I need you in our lives, Silas. I..."

She swallowed. "I think I'm falling in love with you."

*Ach*. Her words were like a soothing caress to his battered heart. To hope...to even consider having a family again after all he'd lost...

Did she have any idea how much her touch affected him? Did she have any idea how much he longed for the words she'd spoken? Their situation was complicated, at best, if not impossible. But then, with God, *all* things were possible. "I must tell you something."

"Okay."

He took a deep breath. He wasn't sure if she was ready for this.

Her countenance changed. She grew serious. "Wait. Don't...don't tell me you're dying. *Please* don't tell me you're dying." Tears filled her eyes. "Silas, why aren't you saying anything? You're scaring me."

"Shh..." He pulled her close and clutched her to his chest. "*Nee*, it is nothing like that."

He felt her relax in his arms, then he leaned back, and looked into her eyes. "Let's sit down."

They moved to the living room, but he didn't dare join her on the couch. That'd be akin to throwing a match on a wood pile already drenched with gasoline. Dangerous.

He folded his hands in front of him. "The day you

told me about Josiah, I prayed to *Der Herr*. I asked Him to show me how to help you, to help me do as He would do."

She nodded, listening intently.

"Then I opened up the Scriptures." He stood and retrieved his Bible from the table. He returned to the chair, then opened it to the passage he'd been pondering. "I was not searching for this. It came up in my daily reading. This is what I read. *A father of the fatherless, and a judge of widows, is God in his holy habitation. God setteth the solitary in families...*"

He looked up.

"What does that mean?" She looked confused.

"It means that God is the One who judges widows, and He is the Righteous Judge. He will care for you and provide for your needs. He is also a Father to the fatherless. He will take care of Bailey and provide for her needs. He takes those who are alone and blesses them with a family. *Gott* knows I have been lonely since *mei fraa* and *boppli* died, and He knows my heart's desire. He has taken care of me and has again provided for my needs." He shifted. "I felt like *Gott* was speaking directly to me. Although you and Bailey were *Englischers* and strangers to me, I sensed *Gott* saying to take you in and care for you. It was almost like He sent the storm just so that you would turn in *here* to find shelter. Here, in the *very* house I hoped to someday raise a family in."

She swallowed. "Wow, Silas. I don't know what to say. How can I argue with that?"

He shrugged.

"And here, I've been thinking that God was *against* me. When in actuality, He's been carving out a path for me, guiding my steps to find the most wonderful man I've ever known." Tears sprung to her eyes. "But how...? I'm not Amish. Isn't that something you have to be born into? ...Or would you become an *Englischer*? ...Or can you even do that sort of thing?"

"If I left the Amish, I would become shunned to my family and my church."

"What does that mean?"

His voice turned somber. This was one thing he never even wished to consider. "It is the worst thing that could happen to an Amish person. It means that I would not be able to eat at their table. I would not be able to sell to them or buy from them. I would be ignored, cut off from my people. The idea is to separate themselves from me completely, so that I will see the error of my ways and come to repentance. It is very serious. And it is disgraceful, not only to me, but to my family also. They would weep for my soul. They would send me letters begging me to return to the church, lest I be in danger of Hell fire."

"I would *never* want that for you, Silas. But you would surely not go to Hell just for leaving your church, right? I don't know that much about God, but I have a hard time believing that everyone who isn't Amish is going to Hell because they are not of that faith."

"According to my Amish church, *jah*. If I was born into the Amish church and made vows to *Der Herr* and did not keep them, then I am in grave danger. That is what they believe. But according to what I read in here"—he tapped his Bible—"that is not what sends one to Hell."

"Then what does?"

"Unbelief."

"You mean, in God?"

"Let me show you." He opened the Bible to the book of John. "*He that believeth on him is not condemned*—this is talking about Jesus Christ—*but he that believeth not is condemned already, because he hath not believed in the name of the only begotten Son of God.*"

He held up his hand. "*Ach*, let me go back and read more so you will understand. Here. *For God so loved the world, that he gave his only begotten Son, that whosoever believeth in him should not perish, but have everlasting life. For God sent not his Son into the world to condemn the world; but that the world through him might be saved. He that believeth on him is not condemned: but he that believeth not is condemned already, because he hath not believed in the name of the only begotten Son of God."*

"So, what church do you have to be a member of? I was always confused about that. Why there are so many churches? How do you know you have the right one?"

"According to what we just read, no specific church. But the Bible does call the body of Christ—those who are saved—the church. So, when you believe in Jesus and trust Him as your Saviour, you become a member of God's church."

"If this is true, then why do people even attend church in a building?"

"Well, the Amish mostly have meetings in homes. Others meet in church buildings. When believers meet together, it is to strengthen and edify each other. Life is difficult and we need others, who believe as we do, to encourage us to continue serving Christ. We also sing songs to God. We give Him glory this way."

"That makes sense, I guess. So, people don't actually go to church because they *have* to."

"The Bible encourages fellowship among believers.

Some may think that they have to, but it is certainly not a requirement to be born again."

"Born again?"

"Yes. When you are saved, you are born into God's family. The only thing necessary for salvation is Jesus. If people fall in love with Jesus, they will *want* to serve Him."

"So, Jesus is kind of like the secret ingredient?"

"Well, if He was the secret ingredient, we'd have to add other ingredients, ain't so? For salvation, Jesus is not the secret ingredient, He is the entire recipe."

"So, if He's all I need, where do I get Him?"

"*Ach*, just ask Him to save you. Here, I'll read it to you so you are not just taking my word for it. For matters as important as this, you need to hear God's Word." He opened his Bible again and handed it to her. "Here, this is Romans chapter ten. Read verses nine and ten."

She took his Bible and read, *"That if thou shalt confess with thy mouth the Lord Jesus, and shalt believe in thine heart that God hath raised him from the dead, thou shalt be saved. For with the heart man believeth unto righteousness; and with the mouth confession is made unto salvation."* She nodded in understanding.

"Okay, now read verse thirteen."

*"For whosoever shall call upon the name of the Lord shall be saved."* She looked up. "Really? That's it? I don't have to like walk twenty miles through the desert barefoot, or offer a burnt sacrifice, or anything?"

He shook his head, amused at her ideas. "Read it again."

*"For whosoever shall call upon the name of the Lord shall be saved."*

"Does that mention anything about walking in the desert?"

"Nope." She laughed. "So, do I need to pray out loud, or how do I do this? How do I become born again?"

He smiled. "There are no special words. God knows your heart. Just confess and believe, like you just read."

"Okay." She took a deep breath then bowed her head. Silas did too. "Dear God, thank You for loving me and for sending Jesus to die for my sins. And thank You, Jesus, for dying on the cross for me. I believe in You and that You rose from the dead and I'm asking You to save me. Amen."

"Amen."

"Was that okay?"

"If it was from your heart, it was perfect."

"I have a question about what we read."

"Which part?"

"Well, the part about 'believeth unto righteousness'. What does that mean?"

"I heard an *Englisch* driver—he was a pastor—explain it like this one time. It made a lot of sense to me and helped me understand." He stared at her. "When we trust Christ, the Bible says that we have the righteousness of Christ. So, in the day when we stand in front of God, He will see us just like He sees Jesus. Sinless. Perfect. Our lives are hid with Christ. So, we are in Christ."

"Oh, wow. Sinless? So, what happens if I sin after I'm born again?"

"Not if, when. You *will* sin in your flesh while you are on earth. When Christ comes for His church, we will receive our new bodies. Those bodies will be without sin. But your spirit is sealed. It is secure."

"That sounds like a really good deal."

"The best deal ever. It's called grace."

"Grace. I like that word." She eyed him and lifted a brow. "Maybe we'll call our daughter that."

His jaw dropped. He couldn't get over the boldness of *Englischers*. "*Ach, jah. Gott* willing."

# THIRTEEN

Silas couldn't erase the smile from his face as he headed back home. Kayla accepted Christ! That meant that they were no longer unequally yoked, according to God's Word. But, unless she decided to join the Amish church, there would be no hope for a marriage between the two of them. Would she even consider it?

*Jah*, she'd joked about marrying him and having *bopplin*, but would she ever *really* consider it? He sure hoped so, because after that kiss, he couldn't imagine not having her in his life. *Ach*, she'd felt so wonderful in his arms. He'd never realized just how much he'd missed having a woman in his life.

After he left Strider in the barn, he headed to the *dawdi haus*. He surveyed the small living area, kitchen, bedroom, and bathroom, remembering the wonderful moments he and Sadie Ann had spent there as husband and wife. She'd only been gone two years. In one way, it felt like just yesterday she'd been in his arms. In another way, it seemed like a lifetime ago.

He thought of the day he'd come home from his construction job two and a half years ago. Sadie Ann's secretive smile told him something was going on, but he'd been clueless. He closed his eyes, recollecting the precious moments.

*"Guess what?" Sadie Ann said.*

*Silas grinned. "You made my favorite meal?"*

*"Nee." She'd come close and pressed against him, then whispered in his ear, "Daed."*

*It had taken a couple of seconds for the word to register. He stepped back, her hands in his, and studied her face. She'd been glowing. "I'm going to be...you are...you are in the familye way?"*

*She smiled and nodded.*

*"Ach, this is the best news!" He bent down and kissed her, his hand resting on her flat stomach. "We have a little one in there right now." He didn't know if he'd been trying to convince himself of the fact or if he was just overwhelmed with awe. Perhaps it had been a little bit of both.*

*He couldn't help it when tears surfaced. A boppli. A testament to their love.*

A knock on the door from the main house snapped him out of his reverie. He realized he had tears in his eyes, even now. He quickly erased their existence, then opened the door.

Paul stood on the other side, a goofy grin on his face. He waltzed in and closed the door behind him. "Alright, *bruder*." He plopped down on Silas's loveseat. "Spill it."

Silas shook his head. Apparently, his brother was not going to give up.

"Come on. Every last detail."

"I'm not telling you anything," Silas insisted.

"*Ach*, so there *is* something to tell! I knew it."

"*Nee*, there's nothing to tell."

"Right. That's why a twenty-minute round-trip took you two hours." His knowing eyes demanded truth. "I'm wondering what you did with the other hour and a half."

"I think your math's a little off."

"My point is the same." He crossed his arms firmly over his chest.

Silas shrugged nonchalantly. "We talked."

Paul's brow shot up. "Talked, huh? And that's it?"

"*Nee*. We prayed too. Kayla accepted Christ." Perhaps shifting the conversation would get his brother's thoughts going in a different direction.

"Uh-huh. Did you kiss her?"

It hadn't worked.

Heat crept up his neck. He wasn't about to share his love life with his little brother. He attempted to keep a straight face. "This conversation is over." He stood and walked to the door.

"I knew it!"

"You know nothing."

"If you didn't kiss her, you would have just said so."

"Out. Now." Silas insisted.

Paul shook his head, not bothering to mask his huge grin. "*Mei bruder's* in *lieb* with an *Englischer.*"

Silas closed the door on his words.

*Jah*, they were true. But it was still none of Paul's business.

He glanced around the room one more time before heading to bed. *Jah*, he was ready to make more *gut* memories—whether it be here in this *dawdi haus* or in a place of his own.

As soon as Silas heard Kayla's car pull into the driveway, he looked up at the clock on the shop wall. Close enough to lunchtime. He dropped the leather reins he'd been repairing and hurried toward the house.

Apparently, Paul had been a step behind him. "What's your hurry, *bruder*?"

"Don't you *ever* mind your own business?"

"Lunch is my business."

"Mine too."

"*Jah*." Paul chuckled. "And you coming to the house the minute she shows up has nothing to do with it?"

"You're here too."

"*Jah*, I want to watch the show."

Silas grunted.

Paul opened the door and motioned Silas in. "After you, lover boy."

Silas felt like tackling his brother to the ground. Perhaps it would have been better just to stay in the barn.

"Oh, good, you two are here," *Mamm* said as they entered. "I was just about to send Martha out to fetch you."

"Is lunch ready?" Paul asked.

"*Jah*. And Kayla and Bailey will be joining us today." Martha locked eyes with Silas.

*Oh, no. Not her too.*

Silas and Paul stopped at the mudroom to wash their hands. Silas surveyed the room until his gaze landed on Kayla.

"*Jah*. Kayla said she'd planned to go into town for

shopping. I asked her to stop by to see if you and *Mamm* wanted to go along." Silas dried his hands, then he and Paul moved to the table to sit down.

"How thoughtful." Silas didn't miss the sarcasm in Paul's voice.

He elbowed his brother.

*Mamm* looked to Kayla. "We could use a trip to the store."

"It's no problem." Kayla smiled. "I'm happy to have you come along if you'd like."

The ladies all took their seats as well and they bowed their heads for the silent prayer.

Kayla took Bailey's hand and encouraged her *dochder* to bow her head too. He wondered if Kayla ever prayed with the little one. Perhaps that was something Silas could incorporate into their lives.

"Is Emily at school?" Bailey asked after the prayer was over.

"*Jah.* She will be home about three. After we come back from grocery shopping."

"Mommy, can I play with Emily when she gets home?"

"May I," Kayla corrected. "And that would be up to Mrs. Miller. She might have plans for Emily."

*Mamm* spoke up. "You may help Emily wash the eggs and gather laundry from the line."

"That sounds like fun." Bailey smiled, then looked to Kayla. "Mommy, can I...*may* I stay here and help Mr. Silas?"

Paul's arm deliberately rubbed Silas's.

Silas ignored him.

"I don't know, sweetheart." She shared glances with Silas. "I'm sure Mr. Silas probably has a lot of work to do. It's probably better if you just come with us."

"But I love Mr. Silas. I want him to be my daddy."

Silas began violently choking on his drink of water. Paul pounded his back. The diversion didn't help the situation, though. Each of his family members stared at him in shock. *Mamm* didn't look happy.

"Bailey," Kayla warned, shaking her head. "We can talk about that later."

"But Mr. Silas was kissing you, Mommy. That means you have to get married, right?"

Silas closed his eyes for a moment. His heartbeat raced. *Ach*, this was not *gut* at all.

"Oh, did he?" Paul's amused voice asked. He turned to Silas and stared, the corner of his lips raised in a satisfied smirk.

*Ach.*

"Yep. For a lo-o-o-ong time." Bailey volunteered.

Paul's finger poked into his side.

"Bailey!" Kayla's voice was clearly flustered. "That's private. We don't talk about those things. Especially not in front of other people."

Silas peeked at her. *Jah*, her face was probably just as pink as his own must be.

"Okay, Mommy." Bailey turned quiet. Silas half felt bad for her.

"I'm sorry," Kayla said. "She doesn't seem to have a filter."

"Oh, no." Paul chuckled. "She can talk as much as she wants."

Silas rammed his brother under the table with his knee, gritting his teeth together. Did he have any idea how much this conversation would upset *Mamm*?

"Paul, *nee*," their mother reprimanded. She speared Silas with a look that could kill.

*Ach*, he would have some explaining to do. He'd likely be banned from ever seeing Kayla again.

Although he respected his mother, that didn't mean he'd honor her wishes. He was a grown man capable of making his own decisions.

Kayla could have died. She *really* needed to have a talk with Bailey.

She sighed. Of course, she couldn't blame a five-year-old for their situation. No, that had been her own fault. If she had *any* idea that Bailey would have walked in while she and Silas had been kissing, she never would have initiated it.

She wished she could understand the exchange going on between Silas and his mother at the moment, but she guessed they spoke in another language for a reason. She was unsure whether they were obscuring the conversation from her or Bailey. Or perhaps both?

His siblings seemed to be listening intently, but his brother wore an amused expression. Paul turned to her and winked.

Kayla shook her head, then looked away. No doubt his brother was a mischievous sort. He apparently lived to tease his older brother. Poor Silas.

She wished they could take a walk and talk about what had just happened, but the likelihood of that occurring now was slim. No, she guessed they would be watched like hawks from now on. No chance of discussing anything.

If his mother hadn't been worried before, she was *definitely* worried now. No doubt she thought Kayla would steal Silas away from his faith and cause him to be shunned. She hated causing turmoil for this family.

# FOURTEEN

Kayla blew out a breath as the four females—herself, Bailey, Mrs. Miller, and Martha—headed toward the town of Madison. Martha spoke with Bailey in the backseat, answering her many questions and teaching her Amish words.

Kayla glanced at Mrs. Miller in the passenger's seat, sitting ramrod straight with a frown etched deep in her face. No doubt she was upset about the exchange at the lunch table. Kayla couldn't blame her. Although she had nowhere near the experience of this older woman, she could imagine what it would be like if some strange boy waltzed in and swept Bailey off her feet in a few years. Kissing her after just having known him a few days.

"What are your intentions toward my son?" Silas's mother demanded. Kayla sensed the hostility in her voice.

She kept her voice low, hoping Mrs. Miller would do the same. It was better if Bailey didn't hear this conversation. Fortunately, she seemed wrapped up in her own conversation with Martha. "I...I don't really have any intentions. I mean, Silas is a good friend, and I do care for him."

"He has had his heart broken. His wife died. I'm guessing he's already told you of this?"

"Yes, he did."

"She was Amish." She folded her hands in her lap. "You and Silas are not good together."

She frowned. "Why not?"

"You are *Englisch*. You do not know our ways."

"But I could learn them." She sighed. "I care deeply for your son. I'm willing to try to become Amish."

"Try? You do not know what you are saying. *Englischers* do not just become Amish."

Honestly, the woman's words hurt. No, she didn't know much about their faith and lifestyle, but wasn't the fact that she'd said she'd be willing to learn enough? "What would it take?"

His mother shook her head. "It will not work. You have a child out-of-wedlock. You would not even be permitted to marry *mei sohn*."

"Don't the Amish believe in forgiveness? In second chances?"

"If you cause Silas to jump the fence, you will ruin his life."

Wow. She got the feeling that his mother *really* didn't like her. "Silas is an adult. I think he should be able to make up his own mind."

"Spoken like a true *Englischer*. The Amish do not just do whatever 'feels' right. Our people submit to our leaders. We follow the *Ordnung*. This will not change for you. Silas is a strong Amish man. You will not sway his loyalties."

If her words were true, she wouldn't be this worried. "I don't understand why you are so against me."

"You are trying to ruin my son's life."

Is that what she truly thought?

"No, I'm not." Kayla felt like crying, but she wouldn't.

"Then leave him be. Love is not selfish. It does what is right for the other person."

"Silas said he thought that it was God's will to care for me and Bailey."

"My son is not thinking correctly. No doubt his mind is *ferhoodled*. It is clear it is lust that leads him, not *Gott*."

The comment felt like a slap across the face, but Kayla tried not to let it faze her. "I assure you, Mrs. Miller, that I don't mean Silas harm. I know you disagree with me, but I think Silas and I could have a good life together if given the opportunity."

"The leaders will not approve it."

She tried to empathize with Silas's mother. But she found it really difficult, seeing as his mother was so dead-set against their relationship. Would she sway Silas? Would he change his mind about them? Kayla hoped not. Because she'd never met anyone like Silas—someone willing to meet her and Bailey's needs even if it meant causing conflict amongst his family and community. Someone caring, selfless, kind, and a whole slew of other positive adjectives. And he was so very handsome. She wondered, though, if it was his looks or who he was that made him attractive to her. She guessed it was probably a mixture of the two.

Mrs. Miller wasn't about to dissuade her. *Nee*, if anything, she was even more determined to make their relationship work.

"Nothing happened, huh?" Paul smirked, lightly pushing Silas's shoulder from behind.

Silas grunted.

"So...not just kissing, but kissing for a lo-o-o-ong time?" Paul imitated Bailey. "Wow, brother, I didn't even know you had it in you." He laughed.

Silas stopped in place, causing Paul to run into him. "Lay off, Paul. What happens between me and Kayla is *our* business. Not yours. Not *Mamm's*. Nobody's. Got it?"

"What are you going to do, *bruder*? The woman is *Englisch*."

Silas turned around now. "Do you think I don't know that?"

"Hey, calm down. I'm teasing."

"I love her. I want to marry her." Saying the words somehow brought an ache to his heart.

"What? You've known her for like two days. You better think that one through."

"I have. I've thought about it. Prayed about it. Searched the Scriptures. All I see is confirmation."

"How is that? *Mamm's* about to pull her hair out."

"I don't need *Mamm's* approval."

"No. But you *do* need the leaders'. And good luck with that."

"I only need God's approval."

"So...what? You're just going to jump the fence? Turn your back on your family and the *g'may*? Leave your entire life because of this woman?"

"*Nee. Der Herr* will make a way."

"How?"

"I do not know yet."

"Silas, you have already been baptized into the church. You must marry an Amish woman." Paul frowned. "Is...is she a widow?"

"*Nee*. She's never been married."

"You know that she will not be permitted to marry you. Even *if* they allow her to become part of the *g'may*, you cannot marry a woman who has conceived a *boppli* with no husband. You know it is not done here. They will not change the *Ordnung* for you."

Silas stared at his brother. "I can go to an *Englisch* judge and get married. Today."

"But you won't. Right?"

Silas shrugged.

"Silas. *Nee*, you need to think about this." Paul's voice rattled with emotion. "Silas, please. Don't leave your family."

*Ach*, he'd never seen his brother so riled up. He almost made Silas believe he'd miss him if he left. That was a shocker. Silas squeezed his brother's shoulder. "I do not plan to leave...but I may have to."

"*Nee*." Paul stomped off toward the house.

Silas decided it would be better to just let him be alone. He swallowed the lump in his throat. His brother had always acted so tough. Who knew that the thought of his older brother leaving could shake him up?

"Whatever happens, *Gott*, please be with my baby brother," he whispered, "And my family."

He didn't know how this was all going to play out, but he did know one thing. He needed to speak with the bishop as soon as possible. And he needed to pray.

# FIFTEEN

Silas had been out working when the women returned from the store. He'd expected Kayla to stay a while so Bailey and Emily would have a chance to play like they'd talked about earlier. But for some reason, she left without even seeking him out to say goodbye.

And that worried him.

Had it been a bad idea to suggest *Mamm* and Martha ride with her to the store? Of course, he hadn't known that his secrets would spill out of the little one's mouth just prior to their departure. Had *Mamm* said something to Kayla? Is that why she'd left in a hurry?

What if she'd gone back to the Yoders' place and was packing her things at this very moment? Silas's heart clenched.

He had no contact information for her. If she left

now, he'd likely never see her and Bailey again. That couldn't happen. He had made a commitment to care for them—he'd been sure and certain it was a calling from *Der Herr*.

He needed to at least go check on them. Talk to Kayla. Make sure everything was all right.

It only took a couple of minutes to hitch up Strider. As he headed out from the barn, *Mamm* stepped out of the house. He pulled the reins tight when he came near where she stood.

"Where are you going?" His mother's expression conveyed her worry.

"To see Kayla."

"I wish you wouldn't."

"I know. But I must." He scratched his beard. "How did the shopping trip go?"

She shrugged. "We got what we needed."

"That's not what I meant. Did Kayla have a *gut* time with you and Martha?"

"I don't suppose so."

Silas ground his teeth together. "Why not? Did you say something to her?"

*Mamm* stood straight. "Only the truth."

"Which is?"

"She is not a *gut* match for you. She will not be accepted into our fellowship."

Silas's heart sank. How could his mother say such hurtful things? And to sweet Kayla, no less?

He shook his head and bit back his uncharitable retort. Instead, he lifted the reins and kissed for Strider to trot out of the driveway. The sooner he left, the better.

"Supper will be ready at six," his mother called out.

It was the last place he wanted to be today. He wouldn't be joining his family for supper tonight. In fact, he didn't know if he'd be returning tonight at all.

"Mommy, Mr. Silas is here!" Bailey called from the open door.

Kayla turned from the cabinet where she'd been putting groceries away. "Are you sure?"

"*Jah*," Bailey tried her Amish word. "For sure."

Kayla smiled, then quickly closed the cabinet door. She'd seen Silas only this afternoon at lunchtime, but it seemed like it had been ages ago. The day had been trying and, to be honest, their shopping excursion couldn't have ended soon enough. It'd been difficult sitting and listening to Mrs. Miller's opinion of her. It had been even more difficult not defending herself or saying something she might regret in the future. Because, like it or not, if she and Silas ever ended up marrying, then Mrs. Miller would be her mother-in-law and Bailey's grandmother. Although she'd attempted to not get offended and remain friendly outwardly, inside the unkind words had stung.

Mostly, because they were true. Being pregnant and alone at sixteen had not been easy by any stretch of the imagination. She'd had to drop out of school and devote all her time to motherhood. Not that she would have done anything differently, she adored her daughter. But it would have been really nice to have someone beside her, who loved and cared for both of them, other than her parents. And now that Silas was here and offering to step into that role, it almost seemed like a dream come true. Especially since she'd learned of Josiah's demise and the death of the fantasy that she'd played out in her mind since she'd first met him.

"Hello?" Silas called from the home's entrance.

"Mr. Silas!"

Kayla walked into the room just in time to see Bailey catapult herself into Silas's arms. She felt like doing the same thing. And maybe a little more.

Silas looked up and eyed her. "*Ach*, you're still here." He grinned.

"Did you expect me to be gone?"

"I hoped not." He frowned. "I heard about the shopping trip."

Kayla blew out a breath and glanced at Bailey. "Sweetheart, why don't you go clean your room now? You need to put your books and doll away like Mommy asked you to earlier."

"But Kathy's still reading."

"Kathy will have to take a nap now. She can finish reading later."

Bailey looked like she would protest, then glanced back and forth to Silas and Kayla. "Okay."

They watched as she skipped off to her room.

"I'm sorry for whatever *mei mamm* might have said."

She'd said plenty, but there was no need for Silas to feel bad about it. Kayla sighed. "It's fine. Don't worry about it."

"My mother can be pretty protective of her family." He removed his hat and placed it on a hook near the door.

"So I've learned."

"She didn't scare you off?"

Kayla stepped close. She reached up and touched his cheek, gazing into his eyes. "I don't scare easy."

He leaned toward her and brushed her lips with his. "*Gut.*"

Kayla closed her eyes and indulged in the too-brief moment.

"*Ach*, let's not get carried away again, *jah*?"

She nodded reluctantly. The truth was, she liked getting carried away with Silas a little too much.

He stepped back. "I've got a surprise for Bailey. I hope it's okay."

"What is it?"

He winked. "You'll see."

"Bailey, come here when you're done. Mr. Silas has a surprise for you," Kayla called in the direction of her room.

Bailey bounded into the room not five seconds later. "A surprise? For me?"

"Yep. *Kumm*. It's in my buggy." Silas led the way, and Kayla and Bailey followed along.

The sound echoed before they could see it.

Bailey beamed. "A kitty!"

Silas opened the door to the carriage to let the small feline out. He glanced at Kayla. "Is this okay?"

She smiled.

"Is it for me? Do I get to keep her?" Bailey held the kitten close and stroked its fur.

"It's a him. And that's up to your *mamm*. But it'll have to stay outside."

"Is it okay, Mommy? Please, please, please say it's okay. I love her already. Him. I love *him* already." Bailey turned to Silas. "What's his name?"

"He doesn't have one yet. It's your job to give him a name—*if* your momma says it's all right."

He eyed Kayla and she nodded.

"What will we feed it?" Bailey was so mesmerized by the kitten, she didn't even look up.

"*Ach*, I forgot food. I'll go call Paul and ask him to bring some by."

"Are you staying a while?" Kayla smiled. "You want to join Bailey and me for dinner and a movie? I even bought popcorn."

"A movie?" He frowned.

Was he even allowed to watch movies? She should have considered that.

"Yeah, I bought one at Walmart. I haven't used my laptop and the battery has a full charge, so a movie will be no problem." She stared at him. "Unless you're not allowed to watch it."

He shrugged. "I'm not allowed to own it myself. And, technically, even the bishop watches television when he's at a restaurant. I've seen him. I think it is probably okay. Spending time with you and Bailey sounds *wunderbaar*." He lightly grazed her fingers with his. It was a small gesture, but that didn't stop anticipation from jolting through her body.

"I think I'll call him Sandy." Bailey examined the kitten, oblivious to the fireworks sparking between her mom and Silas. "Is that name okay for a boy kitty? He looks like the color of the sand at the beach. Don't you think so, Mommy?"

"He does. Sandy sounds like a good name to me." She smiled, then mouthed a thank you to Silas.

His head dipped slightly. "Well, you two get Sandy settled, and I'll go make that phone call. Hopefully, Paul will get the message before it gets too late."

They watched Silas stride off to the phone shanty.

Kayla thought of what she'd prepared for the evening meal. "Do you want to help me with dinner, or would you rather stay out here and play with the kitten?"

"I wanna play with Sandy."

"Okay, but I want you to take him to the side yard and play with him there. I don't want you in the barn or playing by the driveway, okay?"

"Okay, Mommy."

Silas walked back toward the house with a spring in his step. Amazingly, Paul had been at the shanty and answered the phone right away. That rarely happened. He'd be stopping by after dinner with a bag of cat food. Now, though, Silas needed to release Strider and turn him out into the field to graze. Since he didn't plan to leave till late tonight or early morning tomorrow, his horse would be happier if he had a chance to roam free.

Bailey came up behind him after he closed the gate. "Mr. Silas, where will Sandy sleep if he can't live in the house?"

"Outside. Probably in the barn or he'll find a nice sunny spot on the porch."

"You're silly, Mr. Silas."

"I am?" He scratched his beard and laughed. "Why's that?"

"'Cause the sun doesn't shine at night when we're sleeping."

"Cats are nocturnal."

"Is that an Amish word?"

Silas chuckled. "No."

"What does it mean?"

"It just means that they are active more at night and sleep during the day."

"But how can I play with him if he's sleeping?"

"Oh, you'll get to give him plenty of attention. No need to worry about that."

"I wish he could sleep with me."

"Nope. He stays outside, or he'll have to go back home," Silas warned.

Her bottom lip jutted out. "But I love him."

"Well, I love Strider too. What do you think your *mamm* would say if I asked to bring Strider in to sleep in the house?"

She giggled. "She'd tell you no. But Sandy'll get scared by himself."

"He'll be just fine. *Gott* made animals to live outside."

"Oh."

The door squeaked and Silas and Bailey turned their attention toward the house. Kayla poked her head around the screen door. "Are you two hungry? Come wash up. Dinner's ready."

Silas's grin broadened. *Ach*, it almost seemed like the three of them were a real family. Soon, he hoped, they'd all become family indeed.

# SIXTEEN

Silas set down the dish-drying towel the moment he heard the clip-clop of a horse.

"Your *bruder's* here!" Bailey announced from the door.

Silas turned to Kayla. "I don't remember teaching her that word."

"She probably overheard it or learned it from one of your sisters."

"*Ach*, you're right. Seems like she'll be able to pick it up pretty quickly."

"Children have a higher acumen for learning languages than adults do." Kayla finished putting the last dish in the cupboard.

"May I come in?" Paul's voice echoed beyond the front door.

Kayla and Silas both made their way into the front room.

"Perfect timing. We just finished up the dinner dishes," Kayla said.

"I left the cat food on the porch." Paul gestured to the door he'd just walked through.

"Is he going to watch a movie with us too?" Bailey's smile widened.

"A movie, huh?" Paul's brow arched, and he looked from Bailey to Kayla to Silas.

"Yes. Kid-friendly movies are the only kind we watch," Kayla informed him. "But we always choose one that sounds interesting to both of us. It's actually a Hallmark movie."

"I don't know what that is." Paul shrugged then looked to Silas. He shrugged as well.

"Well, I guess you'll just have to find out then." Kayla smiled.

"Do you mind, *bruder*?" Paul eyed Silas.

"It's fine." He nodded.

"*Gut.* Because *Mamm* sent me over here to chaperone you."

"You're kidding."

"Nope."

"She must not know you very well," Silas jabbed.

"Well, she apparently knows *you*," Paul retorted.

"What's that supposed to mean?" Silas chuckled. "I'm the good son."

"I'm afraid you've been dethroned, *bruder*."

Kayla stepped in. "Do either of you know how to make popcorn on the stove? I'm afraid I've only ever made it in the microwave."

"*Jah*." Paul winked. "We'll show you how it's done. Come on, *bruder*, to the kitchen."

Silas reached for Kayla's hand. "*Nee*, I'll just stay here."

Paul grasped Silas's suspender and urged him toward the kitchen. "*Kumm*. See, *this* is why *Mamm* wanted me to chaperone." He let the suspender snap to Silas's back.

"*Ach*, little brothers." Silas shook his head.

Kayla laughed at their exchange, then followed them to the kitchen.

$\infty$

"Mommy, can Sandy watch the movie with us?"

"Remember what Mr. Silas told you? He needs to stay outside."

"But Sandy wants to watch the movie too."

"Honey, Sandy is a kitten. He doesn't care about movies."

"What does he care about then?"

"Well, he likes to play outside and chase things. I'll tell you what. Next time we go to the store, we'll get Sandy some toys to play with."

"I think he would like that."

Kayla's attention was diverted at the sound of hooting and hollering from the kitchen.

Bailey's eyes widened. "What are they doing?"

Kayla laughed. "Being brothers. But it sounds like we better go check on them."

"*Jah*, we should. They sound like they're into mischief."

"What do you know about mischief?"

"Not much."

"Good. Let's keep it that way." She reached for her daughter's hand. "Come on."

Kayla and Bailey stepped into the kitchen just in time to see a handful of popcorn flying through the air.

An 'O' formed on Silas's lips when he noticed them, then his grin widened. "Uh, Paul, we'd better get this mess cleaned up. We wouldn't want Dan Yoder to come home and see this."

Kayla shook her head, surveying the untidiness. But she couldn't suppress the smile that threatened.

"*Ach*, Yoder will never see it." Paul dismissed.

Silas cleared his throat, then reverted to Pennsylvania Dutch. Kayla could only guess what he was saying.

Paul turned around and discovered Kayla and

Bailey standing at the kitchen's entrance. His face blossomed with color. "Uh, *jah*, you're right, *bruder*. We need to do a really *gut* job, otherwise Dan Yoder might not let anyone stay here."

"Is the popcorn about done? We're ready whenever you two are." Kayla smiled.

"Uh, just a few more minutes. You and Bailey can go wait while Paul and I clean up." He looked into the pot and grimaced. "And make more popcorn."

Kayla laughed. "Okay, but we'll be waiting."

Silas snuggled close to Kayla on the couch while the movie credits rolled upward then disappeared off the screen. Bailey had sat between them for half the movie until she dozed off and Silas carried her to her bedroom. *Ach*, this night had been like a dream.

Truth be told, he enjoyed some of the *Englisch* ways. A night like this was something he and Sadie Ann had never experienced.

"Time to go. Morning will come soon enough and we've got a lot to do tomorrow." Paul tapped Silas on the shoulder, then stood from the couch.

Silas growled, then repositioned his arm around Kayla. "*Nee*, I want to stay here tonight," he murmured.

"*Kumm, bruder.* You don't want to make *Mamm* worry any more than she already is."

"I don't want to go," he insisted. He locked eyes with Kayla, his mouth curving into a satiated smile.

"Silas, *nee.*" Paul's tone held warning.

He hated that his little brother was right. Staying here would be a mistake and would cause *Mamm* anxiety. And probably rightly so. His mind didn't seem to work right when he was near Kayla. Was this how Josiah had felt when he'd been around her? He couldn't fault his friend for falling hard for her. Because that was exactly what Silas was doing.

"*Ach*, okay," he finally acquiesced. He hating leaving Kayla. Oh, for the day when he'd be able to stay with her permanently! To hold her in his arms for as long as he desired. To fall asleep and wake up with her beside him. To kiss her goodnight. Every. Single. Night.

*Jah*, he'd need to talk with Jerry Bontrager soon. The sooner the better.

Silas decided to leave his horse and buggy at the Yoders' place, since Paul had agreed to drop him by tomorrow. Paul now flicked the reins, urging his mare along, then glanced at Silas. "You'd better cut ties with her before you end up doing something stupid."

"I won't do anything stupid," Silas insisted.

"I think you actually believe yourself when you say those words. But seeing you two together..." he whistled low.

"And I'm *not* cutting ties with her." He frowned.

"You need to have a care, *bruder*. You're playing with fire."

"I'm not saying that I'm not tempted. But she already has Bailey and, with what happened with Josiah, I just wouldn't do that to her."

"If you say so."

"I do." He lightly punched his brother's arm. "Some of us do have the ability to exercise self-control."

"Maybe. But you're still a man and subject to fall."

"Now you sound like *Mamm*. And I know." He blew out a breath. "I plan to talk to Jerry Bontrager tomorrow."

"Tomorrow? About what?"

"Marrying her."

"You can't be serious, Silas. I thought this was just a fling for you. A fantasy."

"It's not."

"Don't you need to think this through a little more?"

"I already have."

"You're serious."

"*Jah*, I am. I want to be a husband to Kayla and a father to Bailey. Be what Josiah couldn't. I think that is what *Der Herr* would have me to do."

"*Der Herr*?"

"*Jah*. It was as clear as day. I prayed to *Gott* and asked what He would have me do. I asked to be His hands and feet."

"And?"

"Right after I prayed, I opened *Gott's* Word for my daily reading. I read about *Gott* being a father to the fatherless and taking care of widows." He shrugged. "I found my answer. I needed to be a father to Bailey and marry Kayla. But at the time, I had no idea how that would happen since she was an unbeliever."

"And then...what?"

"Well, we had a conversation. I told her about *Der Herr*. I really didn't know if she'd be receptive or not, but after she learned of Josiah's death, something inside her seemed to break. *Gott* used that tragedy, I believe, to bring her to Him."

"Wow. I don't know if I've ever heard anything like that."

"I know. Me neither. But it was like *Der Herr* spoke directly to me. Almost like He was saying, 'This is the way, walk in it.'"

"That's amazing, Silas."

# SEVENTEEN

Silas sat across from Jerry Bontrager. He'd always liked the friendly older man and considered him an advocate, which was why he'd approached him and not the deacon.

"You are asking for an *Englischer* to join in with our people?" His brow shot up. "I admit that this situation does not come up often."

"Is it possible?"

"I think it may be, but it will not be easy." His fingers steepled in front of his chin. "Here is the problem I see. Many years ago, before your family moved into the district, we had a "seeker" who expressed an interest in joining the church. We allowed it, but I fear it was a mistake. This person caused much disunity among the brethren, and we lost several families because of it. It was a difficult time for everyone, and the leaders decided that it would be

151

better to simply disallow anything of the sort again."

"*Ach*, I had heard of a split in the past, but I never heard the details. That is terrible."

"*Jah*, it was. And that is why I do not think the leaders would approve."

Oh, no. He'd feared this could happen but didn't think it actually would. "I'd hoped to marry this woman. Her *dochder* is my best friend's child. He passed away when we were in *Rumspringa*." Silas went on to share the verses he'd read with Jerry Bontrager and explained what he'd believed *Der Herr* had called him to.

"*Rumspringa*? So, this woman and your friend, they were not married?"

"*Nee*. But I am sure he would have married her if he'd known about the *boppli*."

"This will be yet another obstacle before the leaders. Even more than the fact that she's *Englisch*." The bishop frowned. "I am sorry, Silas. But I don't think this is going to work out."

This was not what he'd wanted to hear. What would he tell Kayla? He couldn't let her down. He wouldn't. Not after he'd already made a pledge to oversee her welfare.

*Nee*, he had to try harder. "What if I jumped the fence for a time and married in the *Englisch* world?"

The bishop's mouth hung open, and he shook his head. "*Ach*, Silas! You would consider such a thing? I have never known you to be one to question the ways of our people." Disappointment laced his words.

But there were more important matters at stake. "I would. *Der Herr* has asked me to care for them. It is my duty."

"*Der Herr* guides through your leaders, Silas."

"*Jah*, but He also guides through His Word, ain't so? And the leaders are not always right."

"No, we are not." The bishop frowned. "You are willing to be shunned because of this *Englisch* woman and her child?"

"*Jah*, I am. I do not wish to be shunned, but if that is what is necessary, then I would have no choice."

Jerry Bontrager sighed. "I do not want that for you or your folks. Let me pray about this to see if *Gott* will guide us to a better solution. I will advise you not to mention this to the other leaders just yet."

Silas nodded. "*Denki*, Bishop. I will certainly pray too."

Silas hadn't wanted to say anything to Kayla about his conversation with the bishop until he had something concrete to go on. Right now, they would simply continue with life as usual. Not that life had been usual since Kayla and Bailey arrived. *Nee*, the past few weeks had been anything but. Despite that fact, Silas developed a new routine that included Kayla and Bailey in his daily life. Since he had taken the responsibility of their care upon his shoulders, he made sure to spend an hour or two with them each day, at the very least.

He'd come to enjoy their time together even more than in the beginning. They would usually eat supper together, have a small Bible study, then spend time outdoors. Occasionally, their time would include a movie or a trip to the store or library or park. Silas had pondered a camping trip with just the three of them, as there were two beautiful state parks nearby, but he decided against it to prevent tongues from wagging. Not that they weren't already. But he had no desire to fuel the fires of gossip.

Meanwhile, he waited for the bishop to come up with some sort of solution or suggestion about what steps to take next. Jerry knew Silas was serious about his relationship with Kayla, and if there was a way to prevent him from leaving the church, Jerry would try to find a resolution. He'd been surprised he hadn't received a visit from the deacon yet. That was a *gut* thing. He guessed that the bishop may have had something to do with that.

He brought Emily by a couple of times to play with Bailey, but hesitated to take Kayla and Bailey back to his folks' home. After *Mamm's* reprimand, he didn't want to subject Kayla to any more discouraging words. He'd been a little surprised at his mother because she usually wasn't one to stir the pot. Of course, he'd never been involved with an *Englischer* before either. She was worried, and Silas didn't blame her. She had much to be worried about, as far as Silas and Kayla's relationship went. Because, if they couldn't find a solution within the Amish church, Silas was willing to seek one elsewhere. But for now, he'd be patient and wait for Jerry Bontrager to get back to him.

Love was longsuffering. He could wait. Although the thought of being married to Kayla did excite him, he wasn't in a rush to remarry. He attributed that to abstaining from most physical contact. It was a boundary he realized he needed to set up in order to protect their relationship. They'd moved a little too fast at first, so Silas took a step back. No more prolonged embraces or cuddling on the couch. Contact, except for brief instances, would have to be postponed until they moved closer to their wedding date. And right now, Silas had no idea when that might be.

# EIGHTEEN

Kayla had known the Amish were different from the rest of society, but she never realized *how* different. It seemed absurd, to her thinking, that two fully grown adults would need permission to pursue a relationship. But she was determined to be patient.

Silas had explained many things about the Plain culture to her. She found most of it fascinating, like community support, keeping the old ways, and living off the land. Some things, though, didn't make much sense. Like the use of cars, for example. In their district, they weren't allowed to own a motor vehicle. In the next district over, though, they could own cars for business, but they had to hire someone *Englisch* to drive them. He'd said that some Amish groups even had a designated Amish person from the community who was the driver for that particular district. Then there were some who had permission to drive tractors. And then other more conservative groups who only allowed car travel in case of emergency. And then there were some who could own fancy carriages and others who could only have open-top buggies. Then he explained how the area he was from in Pennsylvania drove gray buggies, but there were also black, white, brown, and yellow carriages too. How was one supposed to keep all that straight? Talk about confusion.

One thing was certain, her perception of the Amish had changed. While they might seem similar from the outside looking in, that was not the case in reality. There seemed to be no two Amish districts alike. Each district's rules were determined by past traditions and changes the leadership agreed to.

Truth be told, she was a little nervous about joining Silas's faith. Not only would it be challenging to adhere to all the rules, but would she fit in? Would she be welcomed by the other women in the community? Silas assured her that she would, once she was baptized, but she still had misgivings. However, she was willing to try for Silas's sake. He would be her support.

After all the time they'd spent together and the relationship they'd been building on daily, she couldn't imagine him not being a part of her and

Bailey's lives. She'd be devastated if his Amish group forbid them to marry and build a family together.

She'd expressed her concerns to Silas, and he always came back with the same answer. "Pray. If it is God's will, He will make a way for us."

So, that's what they'd been doing. When all the answers depended on God's guidance, it was hard not to pray. It had been foreign to her at first because she hadn't grown up knowing much about God, but now she'd become comfortable talking to Someone she couldn't see with her eyes. She no longer denied that it was God's hand that led her to Silas. That was one fact she was now certain of. And if God had brought her this far, she was confident that He would continue to guide her path.

Which reminded her of a verse she'd committed to memory since Silas first showed it to her. *Trust in the Lord with all thine heart, and lean not unto thine own understanding. In all thy ways acknowledge him, and he shall direct thy paths.*

Silas had been keeping himself busy working with his father in construction. If he were going to be providing for a family, he'd need to save up as much money as possible. For the past two months, he'd been sending money to Dan Yoder for the rent of his home. That had been his way to provide for Kayla and Bailey for the time being. Although Kayla thought she'd been paying rent the past two months, Silas had actually been putting it away to return to her later. Because, if his plan didn't work out somehow, she'd need money. But he was determined to make it work. And if it was indeed *Der Herr* who had called him to this life, He would see that everything worked out. Still, Silas didn't plan on having Kayla pay for rent. *Nee*, that was the man's job as the provider.

The moment he realized Jerry Bontrager had arrived, he dropped his sander and went to meet him. He wiped his hands on his work pants and offered his hand to the bishop to shake. "*Guten tag*, Jerry."

The bishop chuckled. "You look like a snowman."

Silas rubbed some of the dust from his face and grinned. "*Jah*, I imagine I probably do."

"Would you like to take a short walk?"

"Sure. Let me tell *Daed* where I'll be."

Silas notified his father, then went to meet the bishop. They walked down the country lane of the property he'd been working for the last few weeks.

The bishop finally spoke. "I have contacted a friend of mine, who is a bishop too. We've discussed your situation at length, and I think we have come up with a solution."

A solution. That sounded promising, didn't it?

"I will send you with a letter to my friend, Judah Hostettler. He is a bishop in Pennsylvania. His district is a bit more lax than our own, and I am confident they will allow this thing. He has had successful results in this area in the past. You and your *Englisch* family will move there for a time while she learns what is necessary to become Amish, goes through instruction, and joins the church. Then, if you wish, I hope you'd move back and join our flock again. The little one could attend our Amish school." He rubbed his white beard. "I'm thinking you'd be willing to do this rather than the alternative you mentioned. Am I correct?"

*Ach*, he'd need to talk to Kayla. This would be a surprise, for sure and certain. "*Jah.*"

But...move away? What about Dan Yoder's home? What about his dreams of owning it? What if he sold it during the time they were in Pennsylvania? He'd have to speak with Brother Yoder as soon as possible. Because, if he was indeed getting married, he'd need a home for his new family. And the Yoders' place would be perfect. For now, though, he could ask *Daed* or one of his brothers to take care of the place while he was gone. Dan Yoder wouldn't have any qualms about that, would he? He surely hoped not.

"And Judah has agreed to house you while you're

there, so you needn't worry about a place to rent. I'm sure he'll put you to work to earn your keep."

Silas sighed in relief. Now, he'd just have to pray that Dan Yoder's home didn't sell while they were away. Perhaps Brother Yoder would be willing to hold it for them.

"Mommy, can I call Mr. Silas my daddy yet?" Bailey looked up from the table where she'd been doing her homework.

"It's 'may I,' sweetheart. And, no, you may not call Mr. Silas your daddy yet because he isn't." Kayla sighed. If, for some reason, things didn't work out with Silas, Bailey would be devastated. Although Kayla was hopeful for their future, nothing had been set in stone yet. And, as it was, they seemed to be in limbo at the moment. They were at the mercy of his bishop and the Amish church. She didn't understand a lot of it, but she respected their ways and trusted Silas to have their best interests in mind. She hoped she hadn't made a mistake in getting Bailey's hopes up. Or getting her own hopes up.

"But I want him to be."

"I know you do, sweetheart. But he isn't your daddy yet."

"Are you and Mr. Silas going to get married?"

"We will see."

"What happened to my other daddy?" Bailey frowned.

Kayla blew out a breath. She knew the question would eventually come, but she still didn't feel prepared to offer an adequate answer. "Your daddy is in Heaven." At least, she *hoped* he was.

"With Jesus? Like Mr. Silas read to us about?

"Uh-huh."

"I like Jesus. Where is Heaven?"

"I guess it's way up in the sky."

"You mean, past the clouds?"

"Past the clouds, the stars, the sun, and the moon. It's too far away to see."

"How did my daddy get way up there?"

Kayla shrugged. "Well, I guess the angels came and got him and took him up there."

"Really? Real angels?"

"Yep. Real angels." She hoped Bailey didn't have too many questions because she was not equipped to answer queries of a spiritual nature. Silas was much more adept at that sort of thing. Although, she'd been learning a lot about the ways of God, she still had a long way to go in her personal understanding of the holy.

Bailey's head shot up. "Mr. Silas is here!" She jumped from the table and ran to the door.

The two of them met him outside. He secured Strider to the hitching post.

Excitement sparkled in his eyes, and she knew something was up. Had he finally heard back from the bishop? Did he have good news?

He bounced on his heels, then leaned close, and whispered in her ear, "Let's talk?"

He crouched down and embraced Bailey. "How was your day?"

"*Gut*!" Bailey kissed his cheek.

Kayla turned to Bailey. "Sweetheart, why don't you go find Sandy? I'm sure Mr. Silas would like to see him."

"Okay." She skipped off around the side of the house.

"Let's sit on the porch swing," Silas suggested.

Kayla led the way and they sat hand-in-hand. "What's going on? You have something to say."

"I do." He smiled. "How do you feel about moving to Pennsylvania for a while?"

Okay, so now she was confused. The only thing she knew about Pennsylvania was that Josiah's family lived there. "Pennsylvania? Why?"

"There is an Amish district there, and the bishop

has agreed to instruct you in the ways of our people. He will allow you to be baptized into the Amish church." He rubbed the top of her hand with his thumb. "And he has agreed to marry us after you join the church."

Kayla's heart soared. "Really?"

"Yep."

"So, they want *me* to move over there? For how long?"

"Not you. Us." He pointed back and forth between them. "*Our family.*"

It felt so good to hear those words.

"I'm not quite sure of all the details yet, but you and Bailey will live with the bishop's family, and I will stay in their *dawdi haus*."

"For how long?" she asked again.

"The baptism ceremony will be in the spring, so hopefully that will be enough time for you to learn our ways and go through the classes. Judah Hostettler also wants to counsel us concerning marriage." Excitement bubbled over in his voice. "We will be married next fall, *Gott* willing."

"Next fall? I was hoping not to have to wait that long."

"*Ach*, it's a little over a year. It will pass quickly."

"Is...is this the district Josiah was from?"

"*Nee.* Different part of the state. But being closer might give us an opportunity to visit them. Or for them to visit us." He briefly squeezed her hand. "I have a very *gut* feeling about this district. The people there sound *wunderbaar*."

"Well, then what are we waiting for? Let's start packing."

"Next week. You will need to sell your car and give away your *Englisch* trappings in the meantime."

Wow. This was all so sudden. She'd already known to expect that, but the reality of it all upon her now caused a slight panic. "There's so much to do."

"Is there something I can help with?"

And there was the Silas she'd come to know and love. Always thoughtful. Always helpful. Always kind. It would be wonderful being married to this man. There was nothing she wouldn't give up to be with him. Letting go of her worldly possessions would be a small sacrifice in comparison to the joy of having Silas in her life. A husband to love. A father for Bailey. A dream come true.

"Yes." She smiled. "I'll need a kiss."

His grin widened and he leaned forward. "I believe I can help with that."

The week following their conversation flew by in a flurry and, before they knew it, they were on their way to Pennsylvania. In just a few more minutes, they'd be arriving in their temporary home town. Butterflies seemed to occupy Kayla's stomach more often than not lately, with all the changes that had been taking place. But they were good changes. She couldn't wait to begin this family with Silas. She couldn't wait for Bailey to be able to officially call Silas "Daddy." She couldn't wait for the three of them to be settled in their own home. But all those things would have to wait at least a little while, until she became Amish.

Upon arriving, they met Bishop Judah Hostettler and his wife, Lydia. They were also introduced to Luke and Brianna Beiler, who would serve as mentors. Brianna had also once been *Englisch* and assimilated into the Amish way of life. She seemed quite happy with her choice, by the look of it. No doubt, Kayla would have a plethora of questions for her.

Kayla had been informed that she'd be attending her first Amish church meeting tomorrow. She had yet to attend a meeting in their Indiana district because Silas had thought it would be better to wait until she was a member. She now wondered how much different the church meetings would be here compared to their own. Silas could fill her in on the details.

While in Indiana, she'd received a visit from Jerry Bontrager, who had asked about her intentions concerning the church. He explained their Ordnung and what would be expected of her as an Amish woman, including her duties as a wife and mother. She had agreed to the church's requirements, and he'd seemed satisfied with her response. He'd been understanding and kind, but astute as well, she'd thought.

Bailey and Emily had agreed to write letters to each other while they were separated. Silas had suggested that. This way, they could keep in touch with the goings-on back at home and the girls would keep each other in mind. It seemed like there would be plenty of opportunity for Bailey to make friends here as well. That boosted Kayla's confidence another notch. She hoped it wouldn't be difficult to leave when it was time to return home. She had a feeling they'd be making some strong attachments here.

"Let's get you settled into your new home, shall we?" It seemed like a lifetime full of adventures twinkled in Judah Hostettler's eyes. No doubt, this man had stories to tell. Perhaps she'd get to hear a few of them while she was there. "Welcome to the Hostettler home."

They walked into the spacious two-story house.

Lydia looked to Kayla and Bailey. "You two will share a room upstairs."

"Thank you for all you're doing. We really appreciate this." Kayla smiled at the older woman.

"This most likely will not be an easy transition for you. Not everyone is cut out for the Amish life."

"What would you say is the most difficult part of being Amish?"

"Shunning those you love when they have gone astray. But there have not been many, and most return to the fold after a time."

"And the others?"

"We pray for their souls. Although, our district does not espouse some of the doctrines that other districts may believe. We excommunicate according to the plain reading of Scripture. If you'd like to learn more about it, you can find it in First Corinthians, chapter five."

"I'm a little familiar with it. Silas has explained it some." She glanced at her husband-to-be and smiled.

Judah Hostettler turned to Silas. "Shall we get you settled in the *dawdi haus*?"

"*Jah*, that sounds *gut*." He looked to Kayla and raised a brow.

The bishop chuckled. "Don't worry. Your *aldi* will be just fine without you. You'll be seeing her at supper tonight."

"I don't think she has any dresses or a prayer *kapp* to wear to meeting tomorrow."

"I have one!" Bailey beamed.

"That's right." Silas smiled. "Emily gave you one of hers. But they wear a different style here in Pennsylvania."

"They do?"

"*Jah*. Do you see Sister Lydia's *kapp*?"

"*Ach*, it's shaped like a heart! I want one of those, Mommy."

Kayla laughed. "We'll see."

Lydia waved at the air in front of her. "I have plenty from when the *kinner* were young. You can wear one of Susie's old ones." She turned to Kayla. "And I'm sure she'd have dresses that will fit you too."

"That would be wonderful. We appreciate that." Kayla nodded graciously.

"*Kumm* now, let's get settled. I'm sure you'd like to rest up a bit before supper." Lydia said, then led the way up the stairs.

Kayla glanced back just in time to see Silas disappear outside with the bishop. She wondered if they'd have any moments of privacy. Just now, she realized she'd miss being at the Yoders' place. She and Silas had plenty of time together when they'd been in Indiana, but now they'd probably only get alone time occasionally. Of course, she was there to learn about the Amish ways. She most likely wouldn't have a whole lot of free time. Soon though, they'd have all the time in the world together. It couldn't come fast enough!

Until attending a church service, Kayla hadn't really realized what a difference in culture there was between the Amish and the *Englisch*. Sure, she understood the variances from the outside—the dress, the horse and buggies, the houses—but seeing what their meetings were like firsthand had absolutely blown her away. She almost felt like she'd stepped back into nineteenth century Europe. The acapella singing, long and slow, reminded her of a Gregorian chant. The preaching, which she hadn't understood, had been in a foreign language. And the service had been a lot longer than she'd expected. She hadn't been used to sitting on the uncomfortable backless wooden benches. The separation of men and women had been interesting as well. She found herself questioning so many things.

Bailey had complained several times, and Kayla couldn't blame her. She wondered if her daughter would make it through the service without crying. Fortunately, she had, and she seemed to be loving the time of fellowship afterwards. That had been a plus.

It wasn't until then that Kayla stepped back and asked herself if she could *really* do this. Could she? It was a huge commitment. For the rest of her life, in fact. If she were honest, she'd admit it had all been a little bit overwhelming.

"Kayla, right?" A woman's voice came from across the table.

"Brianna?" She smiled.

"That's right, you remembered."

"I've been attempting to recall the names of everyone I've met today, but I'm afraid I've already forgotten most of them."

"It'll take some time, for sure. There are a lot of us." She smeared some peanut butter spread on a slice of bread. "What did you think of meeting?"

Kayla blew out a breath and shook her head. "It was quite unexpected."

Brianna laughed. "I know, right? I felt the same way when I first attended one. Of course, I had amnesia and I thought that was the way I'd grown up."

Kayla's mouth dropped open. "You had amnesia? How did *that* happen? That's something I've only seen in movies."

"It is a long story and I'll share it with you someday,

but now I'd like to hear your thoughts."

"I definitely want to hear it. But, yeah, I was pretty blown away. Silas had tried to prepare me, but I don't think anything could have adequately prepared me for that. Seriously."

"Are you having second thoughts about joining?"

"Thoughts? Yes. But I think it's something I can probably get used to. Eventually. It's only twice a month, right?"

"For the most part. And it'll be more fulfilling once you learn the language. The most hectic, I'd say, is when we have to host."

"You mean, at *your* house?"

"Yes. Every family has a turn in the rotation. How often you host depends on how many families there are in the district. We host twice a year."

"Oh, wow. That's something I hadn't thought about."

"You will be learning quite a few new things, trust me on that one."

"I believe you." Kayla shook her head. "How did you do it?"

"Well, support from my family was a big help. And then there was Luke. I would have done anything for him. I still would."

Kayla glanced at Silas, who caught her eye and

grinned. "I know what you mean. I feel like I love Silas more than my heart can contain. It's crazy because we haven't even known each other that long."

"That's how it was with me and Luke too. I mean, he thought he knew me and I thought I'd known him years prior, but when I came to Paradise and we began spending time together, I just knew he was the one." She smiled. "We joke and say that I became Amish by accident, because it was due to an accident and a misunderstanding that I actually ended up here in Pennsylvania. But it was definitely no accident. God knew what He was doing all along."

"Wow. I feel like we have so much in common. I turned into the Yoders' place during a storm. I had no idea where I was, except I knew I was in Indiana. And then Silas came. And well, I hadn't known it then, but I can see now that God had been directing me all along."

Brianna smiled and nodded. "Isn't it amazing? And then you wonder about those things, you know? Like, where would I be now, had I not been in that accident? Where would you be if you hadn't turned in during that storm?"

"God certainly has His own way of doing things."

"Yep. And His thoughts are not our thoughts and vice versa."

"It's like our lives are a bunch of puzzle pieces, and then God comes along and puts the pieces together. And we really can't see the whole picture until the puzzle is complete."

"That's an interesting way to think about it, but it makes perfect sense to me."

"Yeah, it does, doesn't it?" Kayla glanced up as Silas approached.

"You ready to go?" he asked. She'd never tire of gazing into his gorgeous eyes.

"Yes, I'm ready, but we'll need to get Bailey." She stood from the table. "Goodbye, Brianna. It was nice talking with you."

"You too." Brianna waved.

# NINETEEN

Silas and Kayla sat out on the Hostettlers' porch swing, enjoying the crisp evening air and a little alone time. He'd come to cherish these intimate moments when it was just the two of them.

Silas turned to Kayla, hoping she'd like his next words. "I have news."

"What? Good news?" Kayla studied him closely, trailing his arms with her fingers and leaving a trail of sparks in their wake. Her gentle touch always did funny things to him.

"*Jah*. Josiah's folks are going to come to meet you and Bailey this week." *Ach*, it had been so long since he'd last seen his best friend's parents. It would be *wunderbaar* to reconnect with them again. He wondered how they'd been holding up. Even though sudden death was chalked up to Gott's will, losing a love one was always difficult. He knew that good and well. He still experienced moments of grief only he and *Der Herr* were privy to.

She gasped. "Really?"

He nodded. "I think you'll like them."

"Will they like me?"

"You are the *mudder* of their *grossboppli*, of course they'll like you." He attempted a reassuring smile.

"I hope you're right." She worried her lip. "I'm kind of nervous about meeting them. I mean, are they going to judge me or criticize me because I had a child out of wedlock?"

"I don't think so." He rubbed the top of her hand with his thumb. "But even if they do, don't worry about it. We're all sinners. Just because your sin is different from theirs doesn't make them better than you. Nor is the opposite true. We're all on the same plane."

She sucked in a breath. "I'll have to prepare Bailey. Did they say when they're coming?"

"Probably Tuesday."

"Okay. I'll need to have a talk with her tomorrow then."

"Do you want me to be there?"

"Sure. Yeah, I think that would be nice."

He yawned and covered his mouth. "Time to get

some sleep now. Tomorrow will be here before we know it."

After helping with breakfast and getting the laundry on the line Monday morning, Kayla met Silas outside. "Bailey's inside. Do you think we should maybe go for a walk?"

"To share the news with her?"

"Yes." She blew out a breath.

"Let's pray first," Silas suggested.

He always seemed to sense her needs and had God at the forefront of his mind. It appeared to come much more naturally for him than it did for her. But she was glad he offered to pray. She found that releasing her cares to God helped relieve some of her anxiety. Although she still felt she had a lot to learn about the Almighty.

She nodded and bowed her head, knowing Silas preferred to pray silently.

After a moment, he squeezed her hand, signaling the end of his prayer. She finished up her own with a quick amen.

"I'll let Lydia know of our plans and call Bailey outside." She moved to the door and did as she said she would.

Bailey bounced out of the door and straightaway latched on to Silas's hand. "Mommy said we're going to go for a walk."

He smiled. "She's right. Are you ready?"

Bailey turned to her and held her free hand out for Kayla to grasp. "Now, I'm ready."

Silas led them toward the Hostettlers' long driveway.

"Do you remember when we talked about your daddy?" Kayla attempted an amicable tone. She wanted this to be a positive experience for Bailey.

"*Jah*." Bailey glanced at Silas, likely to see if he recognized her Amish word.

Silas smiled down at Bailey and dipped his head.

"The one that's in Heaven with Jesus?"

Kayla nodded. "That's right."

"But I'll have a new daddy soon, ain't so?" She beamed up at Silas.

Silas's laugh was easy. "*Jah*, you will, *Gott* willing."

Kayla forged on. "Well, your daddy's parents are your grandpa and grandma."

"*Grossdawdi* und *Grossmammi*," Silas nodded.

"Grass *dawdi* and Grass *mammi*?" Bailey attempted.

Silas chuckled, then corrected her.

Kayla continued, "They want to meet you. Would you like to meet them too?"

"Are they going all the way to Indiana?"

"No, they are going to come here to the Hostettlers' house. They live in Pennsylvania."

Bailey nodded without hesitation. "I want to meet them too."

Kayla sighed in relief and shared Silas's reassuring glance. "Good. So do I."

"Mommy!" Bailey's voice carried up the stairs, where Kayla currently tucked away fresh laundry in the bureau and closet. "Somebody's here!"

Kayla rushed to the window and peeked out to see a white passenger van. *Josiah's parents.* She inhaled a deep breath, willing her hands to cease their trembling. She glanced into the hand mirror to make sure her *kapp* was on straight, then bolted downstairs.

"Daddy...I mean *Mr. Silas* is hugging the people from the van."

Kayla tried to ignore her jittery nerves and reached for Bailey's hand. "*Kumm.* Let's go say hello to your grandparents."

She briefly looked over her daughter to see if her Amish attire met the district's expectations.

As soon as the two of them stepped outside, a pleasantly-plump woman with silver hair and glasses approached. To Kayla's surprise, she appeared to be about twenty years older than Silas's mother. Oddly, the woman made her think of Mrs. Claus. She buried the thought.

The woman stopped just a few feet in front of them and examined Bailey. Her eyes filled with a rush of tears. "*Ach*, there is no doubt this is my Josiah's *dochder*." She opened her arms wide. "*Kumm* here, precious one."

Kayla whispered in Bailey's ear and nudged her forward. She'd never been shy about meeting strangers.

Bailey's smile widened as the tearful woman embraced her. "Are you my *grossmammi*?"

The woman pulled back. "Yes, you may call me *Mammi* Ada. And your *grossdawdi* is *Dawdi* Alvin."

Bailey gasped. "Like *Alvin and the Chipmunks*?"

*Mammi* Ada looked at Kayla, eyes wide.

"It's a children's TV show," she explained.

*Mammi* Ada nodded.

"Have you seen *Alvin and the Chipmunks*, *Mammi* Ada?" Bailey's smile widened.

"*Nee*, can't say I have." *Mammi* Ada winked at Kayla.

Kayla immediately loved this woman.

"Do you want to watch it with us? We can watch it on my mommy's computer."

"Bailey, Mommy doesn't have a computer anymore.

We're Amish now, remember?" Kayla reminded.

"I like being Amish." Bailey bounced on her toes. "Do you like my Amish dress, *Mammi* Ada?"

*Mammi* Ada nodded, tossing an amused glance in Kayla's direction. "It's nice."

*Dawdi* Alvin walked forward and crouched down in front of Bailey. "Who's this little whipper snapper?"

"Are you *Dawdi* Alvin, like *Alvin and the Chipmunks*?"

He rubbed his beard and glanced up to the sky. Kayla caught the twinkle in his eye. "I'm *Dawdi* Alvin for sure, but I don't have any chipmunks."

Bailey threw her arms around him. "That's okay. You can still be my *grossdawdi*."

He chuckled, patting her back.

Kayla's gaze roamed over the couple, searching for traces of Josiah in their faces. Alvin had contributed his eye color, but Josiah's face had resembled his mother's. A wave of sadness washed over her at the fact that they'd never see Josiah again. What a terrible thing for his parents to have to endure.

"Mister Silas is going to be my daddy!" Bailey exclaimed.

Ada and Alvin shared a brief glance, then turned to Silas. "Josiah would have been happy to hear that you've stepped into his shoes." Alvin shook his hand.

"I'm just glad that Kayla agreed to become Plain."

Alvin pinned Silas with a sober gaze. "It will be *gut* for you, after you lost your *fraa*."

Silas swallowed and nodded.

"Let's go inside," Ada slipped her arm around Kayla's elbow. "And you can tell us all about you and Bailey. Silas says you're from California?"

They led the way into the house, continuing their conversation, and settled down in the Hostettlers' living area. Kayla helped Lydia bring out snacks for their guests.

The next couple of days seemed to fly by and before they knew it, they bid their new-found family goodbye. Alvin and Ada mentioned the possibility of attending Silas and Kayla's wedding in the fall. All in all, they'd had a wonderful visit and Kayla was blessed to get to know Josiah's parents. She couldn't help but wonder how things would have been had Josiah not died. But it was something she'd never know.

With those thoughts aside, she looked forward to becoming Silas's wife. Because, truth be told, if she had a choice between Josiah and Silas now, she'd choose Silas.

# TWENTY

*Several months later...*

Silas had been shocked to learn of some of the differences between this community and his own in Indiana. Kayla would be baptized by immersion? *Ach*, he'd never heard of such a thing in the Amish church! They'd always followed the Amish tradition of kneeling before the congregation inside a member's home. After that, the bishop's wife would remove the woman's head covering and, at the bishop's words, she would feel water trickle down her hair to the back of her neck and the sides of her temples. That was how it had been with Silas when he'd been baptized and with every other Amish church member he'd ever seen. Well, except that he was a man and he didn't wear a prayer *kapp* or require the bishop's wife's assistance. But that was how it

185

would have been for a *maedel*.

Instead, they stood at the edge of Miller's Pond. He watched in amazement as Kayla, and then the other baptismal candidates one-by-one, went into the water with two of the leaders, then were submerged. His district did it differently, but he'd thought this way seemed much more like how they'd done it in the Scriptures during Bible times. This had been something he'd never even considered before.

But none of those things took precedence in his thoughts at the moment. *Nee*, he could only think that now Kayla was an official member of the Amish church, which meant he could marry her with the church's blessing. *Ach*, what a wonderful day indeed!

Disappointment hadn't been a strong enough word to express how Silas felt when his brother Paul called to tell him that Dan Yoder had sold his farm while they'd been in Pennsylvania. Of course, he couldn't blame Brother Yoder for not wanting to wait an entire year for Silas to get his buggies in a row.

With a heavy heart, he hung up the phone call.

*Ach*, where would he and Kayla and Bailey live now? The Yoders' property had been perfect. He hated the fact that he'd have to break the news to

Bailey and Kayla. In truth, he felt like a failure. How would it look if he had to move the three of them into his folks' *dawdi haus*? *Nee*, he didn't want to do that. He didn't want to chance friction between *Mamm* and Kayla. He needed to peruse the real estate ads to see if he could find anything suitable for his soon-to-be family.

Either way, he'd need to tell Kayla. He'd do so on their buggy ride this evening.

Kayla's heart practically overflowed with joy as she sat next to the love of her life. The gentle clip-clop of the horse and buggy enhanced the romantic electric feeling of this late summer evening. In just a few months, she would be Mrs. Silas Miller. Nothing could put a damper on this moment.

"I need to tell you something." Silas heaved a sigh.

Was something wrong?

"About what?"

"I don't know how to say this." He shrugged, his shoulders heavy. "Yoder sold his property."

She took his hand and stroked it gently. "It's okay, Silas."

"*Nee*. We will not have a place to live now." His voice shook with emotion.

"Silas." She stroked his cheek. "Look at me."

He pulled the buggy off the road at the next turn, then offered his undivided attention.

She smiled. "I was hoping it would be a surprise, but apparently Paul can't keep his mouth shut." She laughed. "*I* bought the Yoders' property with the money I had from my parents' life insurance policy. I wanted it to be a surprise wedding gift. My parents would be pleased to know that they provided a home for our family."

Silas's jaw dropped. "Y-you bought it?"

"Yes, *lieb*, the Yoders' property is now the Millers' property. Or it will be once we're married."

"*Ach*, I don't know what to say."

"I hope you're happy."

"I'm beyond happy. It's ours? For real?"

"Yes. I knew how much you loved that place, and Bailey and I really like it too."

"I don't know how to..." He hopped down and hitched the horse to a tree, then he helped Kayla down. He pulled her into the nearest wooded area, without saying a word.

She giggled. "What are we doing?"

"Sorry, I just can't wait another minute." He tugged her near, cradled her head in his hands, and his lips dropped to hers. In a moment, she found her back against a tree as Silas bestowed delicious kisses on her like they hadn't indulged in for months. Warmth permeated her entire being as his strong form pressed against her, igniting a slow-burning fire in her heart that spread with every second. He groaned then forced himself away, his eyes simmering with desire. "I love you, Kayla. I cannot wait to make you my *fraa*. You *know* my heart."

She finally caught her breath. "And you know mine. You have for a long time."

If *this* is what being married to Silas was going to be like, she wished they could say their vows tomorrow.

"We will make a wonderful *gut* family, ain't so?" His thumb trailed her chin.

She wished he'd kiss her like that again. "The best ever."

"*Jah*, I agree. Let's go *home* now?"

"Home?" Her eyes widened. "But we haven't had our wedding yet."

"Let's get married in Indiana. I will talk to Judah to see if he will come home to marry us there. If not, we can stay here a little while longer."

Judah Hostettler's eyes shone with that familiar sparkle. "I've talked to Jerry Bontrager and he has agreed. I will come to Indiana the first week in November and conduct your wedding ceremony."

Silas felt like jumping for joy at Judah's words. "*Ach, denki!*"

"I trust you will provide a place for us to stay?"

"Yes, for sure. You will stay in our new home."

"I look forward to it."

"Me too."

# TWENTY-ONE

Kayla noticed that the mail carrier stopped in front of the mailbox near the road and placed a couple of items inside. It was great being back home again, although they'd had a wonderful time in Pennsylvania. Now that she was officially Amish, Silas's family had seemed much more accepting of her and Bailey. Just yesterday, his *mamm* and sisters had dropped off a plate of cookies and a loaf of bread. They'd stayed for about an hour and talked like she was an old friend. It had been a great feeling to be accepted.

"I'm going to walk to the road and check the mail. Do you want to come with me, Bailey?"

"Nope. I wanna swing with Sandy." Bailey had missed her feline friend while they'd been gone. But Emily had taken good care of him in their absence.

"Okay. I'll be right back then. Stay on the swing."

Kayla walked down the long driveway and breathed in deeply. She loved this new life God had given her. Very soon, she would marry the man of her dreams. They'd all be moved into their property and set up their own household, complete with a little store out front where she could sell whatever she made—be it food or crafts. Silas would be home most of the time if their store and crops brought in enough business. She could spend a thousand years with Silas and never tire of him. What on earth had she done to deserve such a wonderful, God-fearing man who loved her like crazy?

She opened the mailbox. An advertisement wanting them to sell their timberland—that would go into the trash. They would keep their beautiful trees, thank you very much. The latest edition of *The Busy Beaver*—Silas would want to look over that, no doubt. She tucked it under her arm. And the last item seemed to be a greeting card of some sort, addressed to her. She smiled. A love letter from Silas? *Nee*, it was postmarked Pennsylvania. No doubt it was someone in Judah Hostettler's district wishing her and Silas well on their upcoming wedding. Or perhaps a note from Alvin and Ada Beachy. She'd wait and open it when Silas was here so he could share in it as well. Or should she just open it? It was addressed to only her, after all.

She waltzed into the house and slipped the envelope into her Bible but deposited the rest of the mail on the table. She glanced out the window. Where was Bailey?

She hurried to the door then went to the side yard where Silas had tied a rope swing to the large tree. No Bailey. She wouldn't panic.

"Bailey!"

"I'm right here, Mommy." She came around the corner of the house, holding Sandy in her arms. The cat wriggled to break loose of her hold.

"I think Sandy might need to go free for a while. He doesn't look happy."

Bailey's bottom lip jutted out.

"Cats are independent, sweetheart. They like attention sometimes, but not *all* the time."

Bailey sighed and let Sandy down. "Okay."

"Why don't you play with the doll Emily made for you?"

"My Amish doll? Her name is Lyddie, Mommy. Like Mrs. Lydia."

"I'm sure Judah Hostettler's wife will be pleased to hear you named your doll after her."

"She will?"

"Yep. And you can tell her yourself because she and Judah will be arriving tomorrow."

"Yay! Are you and Mr. Silas getting married tomorrow?"

"Not tomorrow. On Thursday."

"And then I'll get to call Mr. Silas my daddy?"

"Yep, he will officially be your daddy then."

"I can't wait!"

"That makes two of us." She nodded toward the house. "Come on, let's go inside. It's a little chilly out here."

As soon as they walked inside, Bailey headed for her bedroom. "I'm going to play with Lyddie and Kathy. They're friends now, just like me and Emily. Except Kathy's still an *Englischer.*"

Kayla chuckled. "Have fun." The door to Bailey's room clicked.

Kayla went into the kitchen to figure out which meals she'd make while the Hostettlers were visiting, then remembered the card addressed to her. She opened her Bible, pulled it out, and opened the flap.

She frowned, attempting to figure out who it was from. *Ach*, Brianna! But no...

Her eyes moved over the page to the name at the bottom. Her jaw dropped. No, it couldn't be!

"No. God?" She whispered as her heart pounded in her chest.

Dear Kayla,

I'm sure this letter comes as a complete shock to you. Surprise, I'm alive! I don't doubt that this revelation stirs up all kinds of feelings for you, and I won't blame you if you hate me.

I didn't know you'd gotten pregnant from our whirlwind romance. To tell the truth, I don't know what I would have done back then if I'd found out. I would have contacted you sooner, but I lost your contact information. Nobody knew it, but I was bent on leaving the Amish at that time in my life and nothing was going to stop me. I went on to pursue higher education and have now graduated from college. I've only learned of our child and your present circumstances recently. My brother is the one who gave me this address. He is sworn to secrecy, so you don't need to worry about anyone finding out about my existence.

Since we have a child together and you're about to get married, I figured I was obligated to at least give you a choice. I'm guessing you're in love with my former best friend. You must be, because I don't know of any other reason you'd willingly join the Amish. Silas is a very good person and you will be happy with him. But, if for whatever reason, you have doubts or you don't really want to marry into the Amish church, I would be willing to help you raise our child. If you're content as you are, then I will walk away and you'll never hear from me again. You can be confident that Silas will be a good father to our child. I'm sorry, I don't even know if it's a boy or a girl.

If you want me in your life, respond to this letter as soon as you receive it. If you don't, then ignore it, get married, and live happily ever after. Whatever you do, do not let anyone read this (especially not Silas) until after you've been married a little while. Don't ask why. Just trust me on this one.

If you ever need to get ahold of me, my brother will have my information. My parents don't know I'm alive and I'd kind of like to keep it that way. No one in the Amish church, with the exception of my brother and now you, knows that I'm alive and well. I know it sounds wrong, but I have my reasons.

I wish you and Silas the best.

Josiah

Kayla folded the letter, her hands trembling. Josiah was alive? She sank down into the chair at the table and dropped her head into her hands. Tears burned her eyes. Emotion threatened to overwhelm her. Why? Why now?

If she ignored this letter, Bailey would never know her biological father. If she didn't, she might lose Silas—the best man she'd ever met. And this letter just went to prove that Silas was a better man than Josiah. He hadn't mentioned that he loved her or wished they could be together. When she, on the other hand, had been pining after him, longing to see him, waiting for his promised letter. The letter that never came. If he'd really cared, wouldn't he have looked her up? Searched for her online? She wouldn't have been that difficult to find. He'd used the word 'obligated.' As though the only reason he'd contacted her at all was because Bailey was his flesh and blood. So, the love they'd shared had been one-sided after all. He had lied, not only to her but to Silas too. She should have known. That was what she'd figured after not hearing from him. She'd been right. And he'd led Silas and Josiah's family and everyone else to believe he was dead. What kind of a person did that?

Yeah. She would respond to Josiah's letter, but only to give him a piece of her mind. He didn't deserve to know their daughter. If he'd cared, wouldn't he have at least asked his brother about his child's gender? He'd said he'd written the letter out of obligation, which meant he *might* have some decency. But as far as Kayla was concerned, Josiah could go to... No, she shook her head. She shouldn't be having thoughts like that. They weren't pleasing to God. What she needed to do was pray for Josiah.

For now, she'd tuck this letter away. She wasn't

sure whether she'd tell Silas about it at all. She wasn't about to ruin her chances of marrying this wonderful honorable man.

# TWENTY-TWO

Never in a million years would Kayla have pictured *this* as her wedding day. She looked down at her blue dress and white apron. Blue? Really? She'd always pictured herself in a long white gown adorned with beads and lace. If she was marrying anyone besides Silas Miller, she'd be disappointed in her unfulfilled fantastical dreams. But she *was* marrying Silas. And this day, even with her blue dress, couldn't be any better. She couldn't be any happier.

White dresses were overrated anyway. How many friends had she known who had their dream wedding only for their marriage to end far too soon? But *her* marriage would be one that lasted a lifetime. It would be one that would stand the test of time. What was a wedding dress anyway? Just something a person wore for a few hours and most likely never again.

White dress or not, this was still the best day ever. Regardless of that fact, she couldn't wait for it to be over. There was still a slight chance Josiah could show up—or someone who knew the truth would disclose his secret—and this whole wonderful dream would come crashing down. That couldn't happen. It. Could. Not. Happen.

*God, please.*

"Kayla, are you all right?"

She brushed away a tear and turned at her beloved's voice. "Yes, I'm fine."

"What is wrong? Why are you trembling?" He came near and caressed her cheek. "*Ach*, you are beautiful."

"Nothing is wrong. This is the best day of my life." She gazed into his eyes. How blessed she'd be to get to wake up to those eyes every morning.

"*Nee*. The day you met Jesus was the best day. This is the second-best day, ain't so?"

She smiled. "You're right."

"I cannot wait to make you my *fraa*." He reached for her hand. "*Kumm*, it is time now."

"Silas, wait." No, she wouldn't tell him. She couldn't.

"What? What is it, *lieb*?"

"Whatever happens, just remember that I love you."

He stopped in his tracks and dropped her hand. His eyes searched hers. "Kayla, what is wrong?"

She shrugged. "I don't know. I just don't want anything to mess this day up."

"*Ach*, you have too many worries. This is *Der Herr's* will for us. And there is nothing or no one that could mess it up."

If only his words were true. She prayed they would be.

"*Kumm*, now. They are waiting for us." He paused. "Unless you are having second thoughts about marrying me."

"Never. Silas, you are the best thing that's ever happened to me."

He shook his head. "*Nee*, Jesus is."

"But I would have never met Jesus if it weren't for you."

He brought her close and kissed her forehead. "I love you and Bailey with all my heart."

She knew his words were the truth. Yes, today would work out just fine. "Let's get married now."

He smiled. "*Jah*, let's do that."

# TWENTY-THREE

"Daddy, Mommy said breakfast will be ready in a couple of minutes!" Bailey hollered from the door.

"Tell your *mamm* I'll be there in just a bit." Silas wiped the perspiration from his brow and grinned. He didn't think he'd ever tire of Bailey calling him Daddy. It was too bad that Josiah had missed out on the joy of having this *wunderbaar* family. Thankfully, though, his friend's misfortune had resulted in Silas's blessing. And it was a blessing he'd never take for granted.

Silas headed out of the barn stall but stopped in his tracks. His head shot up at the unmistakable sound of a vehicle entering their driveway. *Their* driveway. *Ach*, he could hardly believe all the good fortune *Der Herr* had poured out on him. He had a brand-new family with a wife and *dochder* he loved like crazy. He had this home that he'd longed for ever since he could remember. Soon, they'd have the store up and running. And according to Kayla, they just *might* have a little one on the way. It seemed impossible for his life to get any better. His heart was so full, he felt like it might burst.

He set down his pitchfork and went to see who had pulled up. Most likely an *Englisch* customer looking to buy some Amish goods.

The vehicle rolled to a stop and the driver cut the engine. As the person stepped out of the vehicle, Silas felt like the wind had been knocked out of him.

*Josiah? Ach,* it couldn't be! *Nee,* his eyes must be playing tricks on him. Josiah was dead. Yet...it couldn't be, could it?

"Silas." The *Englischer* smiled. "It's me, Joe. Josiah."

Silas's stomach churned. *Nee,* this was not *gut.* Not *gut* at all.

Not that he wasn't glad that his friend wasn't dead. But *how* was he alive? *Why* was he alive? Where had he been all this time? *Ach,* Silas had a million questions.

If Josiah was alive, then...then...*ach,* he didn't know. What would this mean for his new family? After all, Josiah was Bailey's biological father. And what about Kayla? Would she regret marrying him? Would she leave him now that Josiah was alive? And apparently *Englisch*?

If Josiah had shown up just a month earlier, Silas would not have been able to marry Kayla. But what now? What would the leaders say to this new revelation?

"I'm not here to mess up your life, if that's what you're thinking. Did Kayla tell you about my letter?"

He frowned. *Kayla knew?* "Letter?"

"Apparently not." He shook his head. "I wrote her about a month ago."

"*Nee*, I know nothing of this." He grimaced.

"You two *are* married now, right?"

"*Jah*."

"Okay, good. I'd heard she was going to marry you."

"You...you did not come for her?"

"No. I just wanted to get a peek at my kid. I'm moving overseas and I may not ever get another opportunity."

"Bailey and Kayla are in the house."

"Bailey? Like George Bailey?"

He had no idea who George Bailey was. "*Nee*, Bailey is a *maedel*."

"So, I have a daughter. Or, *you* have a daughter, I should say."

"Bailey is six now."

"May I see her? I'd like to meet her. We won't tell her who I am, just that I'm a friend of yours. Is that okay?"

"Let me speak with Kayla first. Wait here."

Silas shook his head. *Ach*, how could this be? He paced to the house, unsure of what he would even say to Kayla. If she'd known about Josiah and she'd kept it from him... *Nee*, she couldn't have known. If she had, she would have never married him. But Josiah had said something about a letter.

"Kayla?" He closed the door behind him. "*Kumm*, we need to talk."

"But breakfast is ready."

"Bailey may eat, but I need you to come here."

She frowned, confusion on her face. "Okay." She set a plate for Bailey and placed eggs and toast on it. "Go ahead and pray and eat, honey. Daddy and I will join you in a little bit."

Silas tapped his foot. He grasped her hand and pulled her into their bedroom, then closed the door behind them. He swallowed and stared into her eyes. "Josiah is here."

Her eyes widened. "Josiah? Is *here*?"

"You do not sound surprised that he is alive."

"I knew. A couple of days before our wedding, I received this." She went to the dresser and pulled out an envelope.

He opened it up and read the words within. "*Ach*. You did not write him back?"

"I did, but only to give him a piece of my mind."

"But if you would have said something…" He shook his head. "Kayla…"

"If I would have said something, we wouldn't have been allowed to marry, right? I wasn't about to let anything mess up our wedding. I don't love Josiah, I love you."

"But the leaders will frown on this, Kayla. They might put you in the *Bann*. You deliberately deceived them. You deceived me." He bit back his disappointment.

"I'm sorry that you're disappointed. But you'd said it was God's will. That He had put us together. That He had made a way for us." Her voice softened. "Please don't be upset. The leaders don't need to find out."

"But he's here. He wants to meet Bailey."

"Tell him no. He doesn't deserve to meet her."

"But she's his *dochder*, Kayla!"

"Silas, don't be upset. Please."

"*Ach*, I'm not angry. I just don't know what to do."

"What does he want? Why did he say he was here?"

"He just wants to see his *dochder*. He's moving out of the country and he might not ever get the chance again."

"Fine. He can meet her, but he will say nothing

about being her father."

"*Jah*, that is what he said. We will just introduce him as my friend." He sighed.

"Silas." She reached up and stroked his beard. "I would say I'm sorry for not telling you, but I'm not. Marrying you made me the happiest woman alive. And nothing is going to change that. Not the Amish church. And certainly not Josiah. I love you. We have our own family now." She placed her hand over her flat abdomen. Soon it would evidence the life within. A life *Der Herr* had blessed their union with.

"*Jah*, I love you too." He intertwined his fingers with hers. "Let's pray."

They bowed their heads, and he uttered a silent prayer. A prayer of protection for his family and for God's guidance.

"Will you introduce them? I don't want to see Josiah." Kayla frowned.

"*Nee*, you need to. This will close the door once and for all."

"You're right. I do need closure, I suppose." She sighed deeply. "Bring him in then, I guess."

Silas briefly spoke with Josiah, who agreed to follow his lead.

"She's eating breakfast," he said, before stepping into the house.

"So, this is our place," Silas announced loud enough to let Kayla know they were inside. He briefly showed Josiah around. "Come into the kitchen and meet my family."

Josiah followed behind him.

"This is my wife, Kayla. And my daughter, Bailey." He gestured to the table, where Bailey ate and Kayla sipped a cup of coffee.

"Hey." Josiah nodded, studying Bailey. He glanced at Kayla. They'd made brief eye contact, then both looked away.

"Would you like some coffee?" Silas offered.

"No, thank you. I need to head on out. Thanks for showing me your place." He lifted a hand toward Kayla and Bailey. "It was nice to meet you two."

"*Gut* to meet you too," Bailey said, between bites.

"You be good for your mommy and daddy, okay?" Josiah smiled.

"Oh, Mommy says I'm a very good girl." She grinned at Kayla.

Silas nodded to Josiah and he followed him back out of the house.

Once outside, Josiah offered his hand to Silas. "So, no hard feelings? I feel bad for tricking you into thinking I was dead, but look on the bright side. You got my woman and my kid." His hand feathered through his *Englisch* hairstyle. "Man, I can't believe how much she looks like me."

"You should not have made us think you died. Was the note real? Did you even go out swimming in the ocean that day?" Silas huffed.

"No. That was just to throw you off. Apparently, it had worked." He smiled, as though he were the most brilliant man alive. "That's why I left all my bags and stuff too. I figured it would be much more believable if I left with just the clothes on my back."

"You really need to let your folks know. It's not right."

Josiah shook his head. "You know they would consider me better off dead than *Englisch*. You remember our friend Michael?"

"*Jah*, he jumped the fence before you disappeared." He and Michael had never been that close. Michael was more of a wild boy, and Silas had tried to keep on the straight and narrow.

"Well, I've kept in touch with him. He had received letters like that. Letters from his folks saying they wished he had died instead of leaving the Amish. They were sure he was doomed to Hell." Josiah chuckled as if it were some joke.

From what Silas knew of Michael, his folks were most likely right. Their friend lived a wicked lifestyle that wasn't pleasing to *Der Herr*. As far as Silas knew, he hadn't found a personal relationship with Jesus. "But Michael had already been baptized into the church. You aren't."

"No."

"You *should* go back. Your folks love you." Silas pled. But if Josiah *did* go back...*ach*.

"Maybe someday."

Silas's heart clenched. Had he actually thought *Der Herr* had impressed on him to make Kayla and Bailey his family? He'd *thought* so. But now he was second-guessing himself. Perhaps it had been his own emotions influencing his thoughts and actions. *Ach*. "Why didn't you come to me before the wedding? I would have walked away. It would have killed me, but I would have done it anyway. This role was rightfully yours."

"Don't you see, Silas? I don't *want* that life. I like doing my own thing...without attachments." Josiah sighed. "You and Kayla are good together. And I have no doubt you'll be a better father to Bailey than I could ever be. It's almost like God put you two together."

Wow.

If that hadn't been confirmation, he didn't know what was. "*Jah. Jah*, He surely did."

# EPILOGUE

*Two years later...*

Bailey bounded through the door. "*Mamm*, guess what? *Onkel* Paul and Emily are coming over for supper tonight. *Aentie* Emily said that I can have one of her new puppies!"

Kayla locked eyes with Silas, who stood behind their daughter. "A puppy, huh?"

"Only if *Mamm* says it's okay," Silas corrected.

"Please, *Mamm*!" Bailey begged.

"We'll have to see. How was school?"

She shrugged. "It was okay. Timmy Stolzfoos was mean to me today."

Silas frowned. "How so?"

"He said *Mamm* was fat."

Kayla gasped, but Silas chuckled. He came near to her and wrapped his arms around her. He looked at

213

Bailey. "Can you keep a secret?"

She nodded.

"*Mamm* isn't fat, she just has a *boppli* inside."

Bailey's eyes widened. "She does? But Emily said *bopplin* come from the stork."

Kayla laughed. "Is that what your parents told her? And she still believes it?"

He chuckled. "Yep."

"You mean, me and Judah are going to have another brother or sister to play with?" Bailey's eyes danced with excitement.

"That's right." Silas leaned close and kissed Kayla's cheek. He nuzzled her neck and whispered in her ear, "And hopefully many more."

The baby's cry called from the bedroom. Kayla smiled. "Speaking of Judah..."

"I'll get him," Bailey declared, then disappeared in short order.

Kayla turned in her husband's arms, and indulged in the kiss she'd been missing since he'd left for work that morning.

"Mm...that was nice." Silas gazed into her eyes, contently holding her in his arms.

A clash of thunder shook the house.

"I didn't even know we were expecting a storm today!" Kayla moved to the window just in time to see a bolt of lightning illuminate the darkening sky.

Silas chuckled. "Welcome to Indiana."

"Oh, I think I received a pretty good introduction to Indiana about three years ago."

"Has it been that long already?"

"That long? I'd say we're making pretty good time, seeing that we've been married two years and have our third child on the way." She laughed.

"*Jah*, you're right." He grinned and pulled her back into his arms. "I'll always be thankful *Der Herr* sent that storm that day. If it weren't for that storm, I'd still be a lonely widower."

"And I'd be a single mom floundering on my own. Now, I'm part of a wonderful community, and I've found the love of my life."

"*Gott* knew what we both needed."

"A storm?" She smiled.

"*Jah*, it seems like we wouldn't have the blessings without the storms, ain't so?" He reached for her hand. "*Kumm*, let's go sit outside on the porch swing and enjoy the light show." He beckoned.

She followed him out the door, and they snuggled on the porch swing. "Who do you suppose He's blessing this time?"

"Maybe he'll bring in a *fraa* for Paul," Silas muttered.

They looked at each other, then laughed. "Nah."

## THE END

Thanks for reading!
Word of mouth is one of the best forms of advertisement. If you enjoyed this book, please consider leaving a review, sharing on social media, and telling your reading friends.


THANK YOU!

# DISCUSSION QUESTIONS

1. In the opening scene, Kayla is attempting to drive through a storm. Have you ever driven through a really bad storm? Have you ever had to pull off the road to find safety?

2. When Silas discovered a stranger in Minister Yoder's home, he felt bad asking her to leave. If you were in a similar situation, how do you think you would have responded?

3. Kayla is intrigued by the simple ways of the Amish. Is there anything about the Amish that is intriguing to you? What?

4. Have you ever used a wringer-washer?

5. When Silas learns the reality of Kayla and Bailey's circumstances, his heart is filled with compassion. Do you think he let his feelings influence his decisions?

6. Silas hadn't been searching for any particular verses, but happened upon one that was relevant to his situation. Has God ever spoken directly to you through His Word?

7. Silas's mother was concerned about her son. Do you feel her reaction was just? Why or why not?

8. Was there ever a time you were angry at God? How did you resolve your anger?

9. When Kayla learns that God's hand had been guiding her all along, he attitude toward God changes. Have you ever acted foolishly as a result of misunderstanding a situation?

10. Paul loves to tease his brother relentlessly. Have you ever had a 'Paul' in your own life?

Dear Reader,

Thanks for reading! I sincerely hope *The Trespasser* touched your heart. This is book One in my brand new *Amish Country Brides* series. I pray each book in the series will be a blessing!

Blessings,

Jennifer Spredemann
*Heart-Touching Amish Fiction*

P.S. Word of mouth is the best advertisement. If you enjoyed this book, please tell a friend.

The next book in the series *The Heartbreaker*
*(Amish Country Brides)*

# THE HEARTBREAKER
## Amish Country Brides

To Miriam Yoder, Michael Eicher is everything she *doesn't* want. Prideful, cocky, arrogant. A defector of the Amish life. And those are just a few of his *qualities*. Why would a *gut* Amish woman like Miriam even consider being his friend again? Especially after what he'd put her through—professing his affection then skipping town. She didn't have the heart to go through that again. It was easier to keep her heart sealed up and hidden away, than to chance vulnerability. And she'd be fool to ever trust Michael again.

Michael has lived most of his youth as a worldly young man. But when he's forced to return home, his eyes are opened to the community he's neglected. Can this self-centered man who'd only lived for himself find something—or someone—greater to live for? Will he be able to convince Miri to give him a second chance?

Made in United States
Troutdale, OR
08/20/2024

22184657R00141